STEEL TRAPP

THE CHALLENGE

ALSO BY RIDLEY PEARSON

The Kingdom Keepers—Disney at Dawn
The Kingdom Keepers—Disney After Dark
Beyond Recognition

WITH DAVE BARRY

Blood Tide
Cave of the Dark Wind
Escape from the Carnivale
Peter and the Secret of Rundoon
Peter and the Shadow Thieves
Peter and the Starcatchers

www.ridleypearson.com

For Paige and Storey and their paternal grandfather, "Bop-Pop" Robert G. Pearson, who made reading a pleasure instead of a requirement

---

ACKNOWLEDGMENTS

Thanks to my editor at Disney, Wendy Lefkon; my Disney publicist, Jennifer Levine; Amy Berkower at Writers House, who is instrumental in all my publishing; Nancy Litzinger, who keeps the office running; Laurel and David Walters, who scour the manuscripts; and to Eric Robertson (retired) of the US Marshals Office, Department of Justice (Seattle), who shared the often secret world of witness protection and helped to create the character of Roland Larson. And special thanks to Dave Barry for reminding me to always keep it simple and make it fun—words to live by.

STEEL TRAPP

THE CHALLENGE

RIDLEY PEARSON

New York
An Imprint of Disney Book Group

Published by Disney Editions, an imprint of Disney Book Group.

For information address Disney Editions,
114 Fifth Avenue, New York, New York 10011-5690.
Printed in the United States of America
First Edition
10 9 8 7 6 5 4 3 2 1
Reinforced binding

Library of Congress Cataloging-in-Publication Data

Pearson, Ridley.
Steel Trapp : the challenge / by Ridley Pearson. -- 1st ed.
p. cm.
Summary: On a two-day train trip to enter his invention in the National Science Competition in Washington, D.C., fourteen-year-old Steven "Steel" Trapp, possessor of a remarkable photographic memory, becomes embroiled in an international plot of kidnapping and bribery that may have links to terrorists.
ISBN-13: 978-1-4231-0640-1
ISBN-10: 1-4231-0640-7
[1. Memory--Fiction. 2. Inventions--Fiction. 3. Adventure and adventurers--Fiction.] I. Title.
PZ7.P323314St 2008
[Fic]--dc22

2007038460

Visit www.disneybooks.com
www.ridleypearson.com

STEEL TRAPP

THE CHALLENGE

PROLOGUE:

MAY 31
OPENING DAY, THE
NATIONAL SCIENCE CHALLENGE
WASHINGTON, D.C.

His heart stopped. . . . It had nothing to do with nerves.

The bleachers surrounding the science challenge's demonstration area teemed with parents and family members, all jostling for better views. In the front rows, reporters had their laptops out, while their colleagues manned TV cameras at the back of the hall, their black lenses staring up at the stage like giant eyeballs.

Exhibition Room B of the Grand Hyatt's convention center had been converted into a kind of basketball arena with a raised stage at one end, bleachers on both sides, and a cordoned-off media area at the opposite end. Prior to introductions—which were to be done alphabetically, making Steven "Steel" Trapp one of the last names to be called—the previous year's winner was to demonstrate his blue-ribbon invention.

Steel shielded his eyes from the bright lights that played down onto him and the other contestants, searching for his mother among the hundreds of guests in the audience. His breath caught, and he gasped aloud as he thought he recognized a face out there.

The foreign woman from the train . . . Spanish or Mexican, with dark hair and brooding, worried, eyes.

The stupid lights from the TV cameras blinded him, and though he did everything he could to block them—short of standing up and leaving the stage—he couldn't be certain that it was her.

The cameras all followed a robot that came out onto the floor—it looked like an emergency cone with a retractable arm—and tried to pick up a glass full of water, but dropped it. The glass broke, the water spilled, and the audience let out a sigh of disappointment.

But quickly, a second robot zoomed out, bounced off a chair, vacuumed up the broken glass, and mopped up the water.

The crowd applauded—the broken glass had been part of the demonstration.

Steel held his hand up to the lights once again: *empty!* Her seat was empty now. He scanned the faces in the crowd, wishing he weren't part of this.

Initially, he had been thrilled to have earned a spot in the National Science Challenge. He'd come here to demonstrate and explain his remote-controlled electronic sniffer. But the events of the past few days had changed all that; he had much more serious concerns now. A human life hung in the balance. Playing with robots seemed foolish.

As the introductions began, he searched the crowd again. He spotted Kaileigh and wondered at the injustice of her being in the bleachers. She belonged onstage with him and the others. Like all girls his age, she looked older than Steel. She had brownish-red hair, green eyes, and some freckles at her cheekbones. But beneath her good looks she was just another geek, and not ashamed to admit it. He was angry about the circumstances that now prevented her from participating.

He finally caught sight of his mother—near the aisle in the second row on his left—her full attention fixed on him. She glanced away quickly when caught, then slowly looked back and met his eyes. Her expression begged him not to be mad at her for staring. But he wasn't mad at her. It was his father who had ticked him off. A week earlier his dad had extended a business trip at the last minute. He was supposed to be the one in the bleachers, not Steel's mom. His dad had bailed on him—bailed on a project he'd helped Steel create. His dad absolutely should have been here. His dad belonged here. His dad was a jerk for missing this. Worse, Steel had had a bad feeling about his dad just before his mom had told him he wasn't going to make it home in time for the trip. A very bad feeling. More than anything, he just wanted to see his dad in person, to talk to him. It felt almost as if . . . but he pushed that horrible thought away, as he had so often this past week.

Steel looked for the mystery woman again, and still there was a gap in the bleachers where she'd been sitting.

One by one, the contestants were introduced. The next kid up to the microphone wore a Hawaiian shirt, a vain attempt to be someone he was not. A nerd is a nerd. Get used to it.

One of the cameras moved at the back of the room. Steel looked in that direction. But it wasn't the camera he saw. Instead, he caught sight of two men, two faces he knew only too well.

The federal agents from Union Station.

He could hardly think.

Oddly enough, they weren't looking at him, but instead, into the crowd. He followed their gaze.

There!

She'd switched seats. The woman with the dark eyes. The woman with the foreign accent from the train platform in Chicago. The woman who'd started all the trouble with the briefcase in the first place.

He had no doubts now: it was her, sitting only a few rows behind Steel's mother.

To his horror, he watched as his mother also spotted the agents. She got up from her seat in a hurry and worked her way down the aisle and—steaming mad, there was no mistaking that look of hers—marched toward the taller agent. Steel had to stop her.

He stood up.

An older kid next to him pushed him down and said, "Stay in your seat, Einstein. It's not your turn, unless your name is Annie Delmer."

Steel's belly twisted into an unforgiving knot.

There was only one explanation for the woman's being here: she was looking for the briefcase.

FRIDAY, MAY 13,
TWO WEEKS BEFORE
THE CHALLENGE

Kyle Trapp's heart soared. He loved flying, and he was currently piloting a single-engine Cessna five thousand feet above Lake Michigan. The sky shone blue above lake water of cinnamon gray. Kyle possessed information vital to the investigation, a secret so sensitive that he couldn't trust telephones or e-mail; he could deliver it only in person. He checked his watch: another two hours.

The smell hit him first: a nasty, bitter taste at the back of his throat. It took him just seconds to realize it was electrical. The plane's avionics—the flight instruments—all went dark simultaneously. He tapped the various dials. Nothing. Without electronics, he couldn't set the plane to fly itself, so he steadied the yoke and double-checked the fuses by running his hand over them, feeling for one that might be sticking out. Again, nothing.

The motor coughed and sputtered, then caught back to life.

He stayed calm, as he'd been trained, and tried to determine the cause, and therefore the solution. He pulled his laminated checklists out of the door's side pocket, flipped through the pages, and tried some circuit breakers, to no effect.

Every electrical instrument on the plane's console was dead. Only the vacuum-assisted devices still worked: the altitude indicator and the compass.

He pulled a backup radio out of his flight bag, switched it on, and tuned to an emergency frequency.

A new smell: burning oil.

The motor was on fire.

Coughing, he set the radio down on the copilot seat and twisted open the small vent, letting in much-needed fresh air.

The altitude indicator informed him the plane was slipping to the right. Seeing this, he jerked the wheel too strongly, an amateur mistake. The radio slipped off the seat and banged out of sight.

A haze filled the cockpit, despite the vent. He coughed and gagged as it grew thicker.

He reached under his seat for the fire extinguisher—but where to aim? He couldn't *see* any fire, only smell it.

With a fire raging on the other side of the console, he couldn't use the supplemental oxygen without risk of causing an explosion.

The fuselage began to shudder. The plane picked up speed, now in a steep dive.

Gagging and coughing, he pulled on the yoke, worked the rudder, but everything felt wrong. It wasn't just a dive, it was a spiral. The plane sank faster and faster, the whine of the wind in the side vent now a scream. *What to do?*

He knew how to pull out of a "dead man's spiral"—he'd not only studied it during his training, he'd practiced it—so why couldn't he remember now? Then he realized why: his head was faint. He wasn't thinking clearly. He was on the verge of passing out.

The motor coughed once more, and died.

His head swooned. He couldn't see, couldn't stop coughing, couldn't think. And yet he pulled the plane out of the spiral. He leveled off and spotted a tiny island up ahead. Or was that the shore?

Holding the yoke one-handed, he unfastened his harness and lunged across the passenger seat, his right hand frantically searching for the fallen handheld radio. He felt something . . . *but no, that wasn't it*. Again his fingers touched cold metal—but this was some part of the seat. *Not the radio.*

One last try: he had it.

He depressed the button on the side of the radio, raised it to his dry lips, and managed to get out one word, over and over like a prayer:

"Mayday . . . Mayday . . . Mayday . . ."

He forced his door open, battling the air pressure holding it shut. For a moment, the cockpit cleared, and he could see.

Sand . . . flat sand . . .

He set the flaps and gripped the yoke with both hands.

1.

THURSDAY, MAY 29, TWO DAYS BEFORE THE NATIONAL SCIENCE CHALLENGE

"FIDOE stands for Fully Integrated Digital Odor Evaluator. It is to robots what a bloodhound is to the world of dogs. I recycled parts from the MITZ-AI-5, capitalizing on momentum components to conserve battery power." Steel's voice faltered and cracked above the steady hum of the train car's ventilation system. The train stood at platform seven in Chicago's Union Station, awaiting its scheduled departure.

"I'm not saying I understand it the way your father does, but you delivered it well," Judy Trapp said to her son.

"I can't do this."

"Of course you can. You read that *very* well. You'll do fine. Read some more."

"Later," he said. "If that's all right."

"Later is okay," she said, "as long as we rehearse the whole talk. It's going to be different with an audience. The more you practice, the easier it will be when the time comes."

He knew she wouldn't push him—his mother was in awe of his brain power. She was always defending him to his more demanding father. She pretty much gave him whatever he wanted whenever he wanted it. He didn't overuse this power—or tried not to—but he knew she was there when he needed her.

"Can I go check on Cairo?" Steel asked. It seemed unfair that their dog had to ride in the baggage compartment.

"Ste . . . ven!" She used his given name rarely, but when she did, it was typically in a tone of voice that informed him he was on dangerous ground. The nickname, Steel, had been the work of his first-grade teacher, who, astonished by his photographic memory, had said in front of all his friends that he had "a mind like a steel trap"—making a play on words with his last name. But the nickname had been picked up by his classmates and had stuck, eventually finding its way into his home.

The scolding had a bit of his father in the sound of it, and for a moment it took Steel aback. Truth was, his mother was out of her element taking him to the National Science Challenge.

She didn't belong here; she never paid any attention to his science projects. *So why now?* It occurred to him that she was there in place of his father because his parents were having problems. He wasn't blind. He'd seen plenty of families self-destruct. But his own? It seemed inconceivable. Still . . . *the way she was acting* . . .

"Ah, come on, Mom. Please?"

"You can visit Cairo only if the conductor is free to help you. He has to unlock the baggage car. You heard him. It wasn't my idea."

She used that excuse whenever handy: it was always somebody else's idea if it amounted to denying him something.

He let his dark bangs fall over his eyes and brushed them away in time to give her the Steel look: a hint of childish sincerity, a touch of playfulness. Cairo gave him the same look when she wanted to go outside and play with her rope toy.

His mother didn't respond in her usual way, so he sneaked a look at himself in the reflection off the window glass: his ears stuck out a little far; his new glasses looked too big—he hated them. His mouth looked small and his nose too big, all because of those stupid glasses. His mother claimed his face was "growing into itself," whatever that meant. But combined with his stringy long legs and straw-thin arms, there wasn't much to grow into. Sadly, he thought he looked like the geek he was. He was the walking stereotype of the human nerd, and there wasn't anything he could do about it. If he got zits on top of it all, he was going to go live on an uninhabited island.

"Seventy-eight," he said.

"Seventy-eight what?" she asked. She always got suckered into these tricks of his, and he felt bad for messing with her, but he wanted to visit Cairo; if she wasn't going to let him, then he was going to mess with her.

"The train car," he said, "seats seventy-eight passengers. There's space for two wheelchairs." She looked at him like he was speaking a foreign language. He went on to recite every statistic about the train that he'd read off an Internet site two weeks earlier. He loved to impress her.

"Wow! You are truly amazing," she said. So proud. So very proud. She couldn't help herself.

"I read it on the Internet." Steel had a photographic memory and total recall. He needed to read something only once, and even a year later he could recite it by heart. That was his secret: it wasn't that he was so smart, he just never forgot anything. People assumed the two things were the same—but he knew differently. Smart was knowing everything *and* possessing the creativity to see beyond what you knew. His father was like that. His father had the gift.

"I could look for a conductor. If I found one, and he agreed to let me in, then I could go check on Cairo. What's wrong with that?"

She lowered her voice. "She isn't supposed to even be here, Steel, you know that. I fibbed to get them to allow her to come along. I don't want to push it."

"You think the conductor cares about any of that?" Steel asked. "I'll bet they love having a dog on board. Rules don't always make sense, Mom. Everybody knows that, even the people who make them." He tried to work this logic on her whenever possible, since most of the rules he had to live by were hers and his father's. He could tangle her up pretty well when he really put his mind to it. She wasn't a bad debater, but her heart often got in her way.

"Well, it wasn't me who made this rule," she said. "It was the conductor, and we're going to obey it. You can look for a conductor once the train is a half hour or so out of the city. The conductors have things to do, don't forget, other than helping little boys go pet their dogs."

"I'm not a little boy." Steel gazed out the window at the steady stream of passengers arriving on the platform. His mind wandered to Cairo and what she must be going through. A cross between a German shepherd and a saluki hound, she was a decent-size dog with a dark blond coat and "feathering" on the backs of her legs. Her travel crate was big, but she was the type of dog that liked to run around and play. She had to be going crazy. He looked down and studied the page of his talk, taking a mental picture of it. Immediately it was committed to memory. He felt tempted to show off and recite it for his mom, but he thought he might wait and use it as a negotiating tool.

Her cell phone rang and she answered it. This was good: when she got into a good, solid phone call she mentally left the room.

He considered making a break for the baggage car. She wouldn't follow, wouldn't stop him. Probably wouldn't even notice. And if she did notice, she wouldn't make a scene. But he'd pay later, and it was going to be a long trip. He wasn't crazy about the idea of spending nearly two days with his mother mad at him. Better not push it.

"Hold on, just a minute," she said, cupping the

cell phone. "Steel, I'm going to take this by the restroom. It's private."

"Is it Dad?"

"No. Just private."

She headed down the aisle and began talking again. Something weird was up: she didn't usually keep secrets from Steel.

He looked down the central aisle at all the people settling in. He knew which head belonged in what seat. Had it memorized. It was just the way his mind worked; some people remembered songs or dialogue from films, Steel remembered anything and everything he saw: the plays of a football game, a math equation three lines long, or the backs of heads of seventy-six people in a train car.

So when the pretty woman with the dark hair and sunglasses left her seat and headed off the train and out onto the platform, Steel quickly jumped up, following her window to window, paralleling her movement *away* from the direction of his mother.

Mid car he looked up into the overhead rack and saw what he could picture so well: the briefcase. He'd seen her carry it on board, and now she'd left without it. He reached up. He found himself out on the platform, pursuing her. He struggled against the tide of late arrivals, the woman's briefcase in hand.

"Hey! Lady!" he called out in his croaking, cracking voice. It was an embarrassment to even talk. Why couldn't he be a year older right now? He hoisted the briefcase over his head—the thing was light as a feather.

She had to be ignoring him, for she certainly could hear him: everyone was looking in his direction.

"Excuse me! Lady!" he shouted even louder, still hoisting the briefcase.

He caught up to her at last.

"Lady! Lady! Your bag!"

She stopped and turned slowly, as if she didn't want to turn around, as if she were one of those monsters in a horror movie that had the face of the devil. But it wasn't true: she had a nice face. Spanish, maybe. Her eyes widened when she saw what he carried. "What are you doing?" She couldn't take her eyes off the briefcase. "What the"—she caught herself—"*heck* are you doing with that?"

Winded, Steel blurted out at her, which was pretty much the way he talked, winded or not. Talking with anyone other than his mom and dad, his mouth became a bottleneck, an impediment to the speed at which his mind worked. The faster he spoke, the fewer words piled up waiting to get out, so he spoke very fast.

"You left this—and I saw you—and I started to follow—and I tried to catch up because I thought you'd forgotten it—and the train's going to leave any minute now—and that would leave you *off* the train and the briefcase *on* the train—and so here I am." He pushed the case toward her. She didn't accept it, raising her arms.

"Not mine."

"Yeah. Yours. You carried it on the train not five minutes ago. I saw you. I'm six rows behind you." He squinted. "You were seven rows from the front, aisle seat, left side. You have a red squishy thing holding your hair in a ponytail. When you came in, you put the briefcase in the overhead rack and sat down." Again he encouraged the briefcase toward her.

Her face remained impassive. "I'm sure you are mistaken."

Steel knew himself to be many things—precocious, overconfident, intelligent, geeky—but not mistaken. Not now. Not ever. "No, actually. I'm never wrong." He stated it for her just like that. He got a rise out of her, too. She took a step back. He said, "You boarded with this briefcase. You put it up in the overhead rack, and you left the train without it. You don't strike me as a terrorist, and it isn't heavy enough to contain a bomb. . . ."

She looked him up and down. "You have me confused with someone else, young man. And that means at the moment you've stolen someone's briefcase, and I do not imagine this person will be happy about that."

"You're wrong," he said. "You're lying to me. Why are you lying?"

Her impassive face broke, and she looked clearly uncomfortable. She glanced around the busy platform.

He repeated, "I saw you. I am *not* making a mistake. I don't make this kind of mistake."

"Well, you have made one now. You will miss the train," she said. "Thank you for trying to help me, but honestly, *it is not mine.*" She delivered this with such overbearing, angry determination that he didn't challenge her. Never mind that she was flat-out lying.

"Whatever," he said.

"Good luck at the challenge," she said. She answered his puzzled expression by pointing to his sweatshirt. It bore the logo for the National Science Challenge, Washington, D.C., and the dates June 6–8.

"Oh, yeah," he said. She'd made her point: he wasn't the only attentive one.

"Good-bye." She said this in a definitive, final way. No room for discussion. She turned and hurried away.

Steel reentered the train car lost in thought. He

absolutely knew what he'd seen. Wasn't going to hear otherwise. So why had she lied?

He was about to return the briefcase to the overhead rack when he spotted his mother standing by their seats, nearly shaking from anger.

He walked down the aisle, past passengers readying for the trip, and joined her.

"Explain yourself, young man."

When she was mad at him—really mad, like this—she scared him. He knew at these times he held no power over her, and that scared him even more.

He explained himself. What had started out as a good deed had ended in a confused muddle. His mother knew to trust his visual memory. She didn't question for a moment if he was sure what he'd seen. She'd lived with him for fourteen years.

"Well," she said, "I can hardly be mad at you for attempting to do a good deed, now can I?" She glanced up the aisle.

"I think we should mention it to a conductor. Unattended bags . . . it's no different from an airport."

"It's not like she's a terrorist or something."

"Just the same, he'll know what to do. We'll mention it to the conductor," she said.

And that was that.

2.

Natalie Shufman reached Union Station's great hall and looked around for her handler. She bristled at the idea of being babysat, but that was how these people did things. They took extreme care to isolate one thing from another, one person from another. She could pretty much guess who the briefcase was intended for, but she would never be told. If any one of them were arrested or taken into custody, he or she would have so little of the big picture as to be useless to authorities.

Sounds of track announcements echoed off the high ceiling. People milled about. Spotting him at last—recognizing the intense though common enough face beneath short-cropped hair—she headed over to him. At twenty-eight, he was slightly older than she was, and she feared him, for he was no one to mess with. None of these people were. Had they not rescued her from her stupidity—the possibility of a drug charge they still held over her—she wouldn't have been a part of any of this. But here she was, and there was no undoing it.

"So?" he said.

"I should have just given it straight to our guy."

"It's not how it works. No one is to see his face. It went okay?"

"Why is he doing this, anyway?" she asked, inferring she already knew who was the intended recipient. "Why would a guy as high up as he is play the part of a lowly courier? It doesn't make sense."

"We don't question something like that." It was a stern warning, but she didn't take it to heart.

"It has to be something hugely important or hugely valuable. What do you suppose it is?"

"I asked you if it went okay," he said pointedly.

She considered not telling him, but he might have been watching—this could be some sort of test.

"There was a boy."

He glanced at her, and she felt his intensity.

She said, "He saw me leave the briefcase and he came after me with it. Out onto the platform."

He seethed next to her, blood coloring his face in anger. "Go on."

She spoke quickly, hoping the explanation might satisfy him. "I told him he was mistaken. That it wasn't mine and he should put it back where he'd found it. I'm sure he did."

"Did you get his name?"

"His name? No, of course not. I told him to put it back, and that was the end of it."

"Describe him to me."

"Why?"

He stared silently at her, and she felt he might hurt her if she didn't do as he said.

"Thirteen, fourteen. Thin. Kind of nerdy. He's wearing a sweatshirt for the National Science Challenge. That's why he's going to Washington—this challenge. He's not going to be a problem. It wasn't anything. Really. I shouldn't have mentioned it."

"No, you did right. Go on. Get outta here. Head back as planned," he said. "You can go."

As she walked away from him, her stomach turned. Why had she mentioned the boy? What had she started?

She thought of the train ticket in her pocket. She checked the huge board listing all the trains and tracks, the departures and arrivals.

The train to Washington was still in the station.

What if they now planned to hurt the boy? Wouldn't that make whatever happened to him her fault?

She eyed the gate to track seven, then stole a glance back at the man she'd just spoken to. He was talking on his cell phone, his back turned to the gate.

If she hurried, she might have a chance.

3.

"Wait a second! Back it up," Roland Larson instructed. He and Trill Hampton, both United States marshals assigned to the Fugitive Apprehension Task Force, occupied uncomfortable chairs in a cigarette-soured windowless room with TERMINAL SECURITY written on its door. Between them sat a security guard who controlled the video.

Hampton, an African American with a kind face and a football player's neck, smacked loudly as he chewed french fries laden with ketchup, withdrawn one by one from an oily paper bag. Larson battled impatience. He had a rugged face, sharp blue eyes, and dirty-blond hair. He was too big for the chair.

Chicago's Union Station had trains coming and going at all hours. As part of the U.S. Marshals

Fugitive Apprehension Task Force, Larson's present assignment was to track down and capture a suspected gang leader, a man believed to have ties to a terrorism cell in Chicago. A joint FBI and Secret Service investigation had uncovered the gang's connection to a series of minor bank robberies. It was now believed that stolen money had reached the terrorist cell. The disappearance of a small plane over Lake Michigan had given rise to the discovery that a much bigger plan to raise money for the terrorists was currently underway. Larson had never seen the man he was after. There were no existing photographs of him. All Larson had was a vague description provided by an undercover agent: broad-shouldered, five feet eleven inches, intense eyes, and a possible name that could easily be an alias: Aaron Grym. It wasn't much to go on.

They were reviewing train station surveillance video. The known gang member was approached by a woman, possibly in her mid-twenties. Her face had not been caught by the overhead camera. The two spoke with an undeniable intensity. Then the gang member used his cell phone, and shortly thereafter left the station.

"The only train boarding at that time is the overnight to Washington." The station's security man pointed to the television monitor. The smell in the room was mostly his. "There is one that leaves for St. Louis ten minutes later. Another for Minneapolis on the half hour. But at that time, it is Washington, D.C."

"Can you give us any platform cameras you might have?"

It took the security guard a few minutes to organize himself. Hampton finished the french fries. Finally the video started, and Larson went back to watching the small screen. The camera looked out from the terminal down track seven's long platform. The train to Washington, D.C., was to the right of the platform.

"There! Stop the tape!" Larson shouted, a little too loudly for the small room. Of the two dozen passengers frozen in black-and-white, all but one had their backs to the camera as they headed toward the train. The only one facing them was a woman—a woman wearing jeans and looking like the same woman who'd been seen with the gang member out in the terminal. The woman was walking *away* from the train.

Hampton sat up in his chair. "She's leaving."

"Yeah," said Larson. "I noticed."

"She saw someone off?" Hampton inquired.

The security guy said, "Only ticketed passengers are allowed on the platform. If she's on the platform, then she bought a ticket."

Larson said, "She decided not to take the trip."

"It happens," the guy said. "Plans change. Schedules change. People get sick."

"Madrid," Hampton muttered.

A few years earlier, terrorists had blown up a commuter train in Madrid, Spain, killing hundreds of innocent passengers.

"London," Larson said. Two summers earlier, bombs had exploded in the London Underground.

"I want to see her when and if she *entered* the train," Larson advised the security man. "Back it up."

Hampton reached for the desk phone because cell reception was poor in this basement office. He asked someone on the other end to arrange transportation to Toledo—the Washington train's next stop. He knew in advance that this was what Larson would want. They worked well as a team.

"Freeze it!" Larson shouted, again too loudly. He pointed out the same woman, now walking *toward* the train on a video shot well before the other one. "That's her!"

"No it's not," Hampton said, cupping the phone. "Same clothes, but that woman's carrying a briefcase. The woman we saw wasn't—" but he caught himself.

"—carrying a briefcase," Larson finished for him. "Because she left it on the train."

"I know what you guys are thinking," the security man said. "But if there had been a bomb in that briefcase, we'd have caught it. Forget about it."

"What about money?" Hampton asked. "What about a pile of money being delivered to the wrong people?"

"We want to follow that bag," Larson said. "It could lead us to our man."

Hampton still had the person on the line. He said, "We're going to need a private jet, and you gotta get a VCR on board." He checked his watch. "Have it standing by in forty minutes." He hung up.

Larson told the security man, "We're going to need every surveillance tape from every camera in the station from two hours before that train departed. Find a box. We're taking them all with us."

"When does the train arrive in Toledo?" Hampton asked the bewildered security man.

The man typed some information into a laptop, ran his finger along the screen, and said behind a defeated face, "Government jet or not . . . it'll take a miracle to catch that train."

"Not a problem," Larson said, coming to his feet.

Hampton pointed first to Larson and then to himself. "Miracles-R-Us."

4.

Aaron Grym fought the temptation to speak to the boy and his mother, and reclaim the briefcase. He wasn't sure how it might play out, and he didn't want to draw attention to himself, to give them a face to remember. Yet he needed that bag.

At some point the kid was certain to put the briefcase back where he'd found it. At the very least, the mother and son would eventually fall asleep. It was a long way to Washington, D.C. Opportunity would present itself. He would wait it out.

In the meantime, he would change his looks. The backpack in the overhead rack was filled with clothing and various elements to help with his disguise: several wigs, makeup, contact lenses. Nothing that took too long to apply. He'd learned the art of disguise from a community center in his neighborhood that had offered acting classes. He'd spent two summers at the center, his last playing Tony in *West Side Story*. Now he would *become* Tony. Life imitating art.

People could be after him. People with badges. People with radios. A lot of people. He kept firmly in mind that an informer had penetrated his organization's ranks. There was no way to know how much of what they had planned had been compromised—including this train ride.

If possible, he'd get the briefcase from the boy ahead of the Toledo stop. Disembarking the train there, he'd find another way to reach Washington.

Temptation pulled at him to make a simple introduction to the boy and his mother: "I believe you have my briefcase." The boy would bring up having seen the woman with the case. "Ah, you mean my wife!" he could say. "Yes. She had to leave suddenly. Her mother. An illness. I have a key to the briefcase. Isn't that proof enough?"

If they called his bluff, if they made him open the briefcase, then he would have to take care of them before Toledo. The expression "Cancel their tickets" crossed his mind and caused him to smile.

He and his group had been told that Homeland

Security had installed hidden wireless security cameras on all Amtrak trains as well as most commuter lines. Wireless, so the cameras could be monitored and studied from a land-based office.

He didn't know if it was true or not, but he kept his head down as much as possible. It seemed doubtful that the cops or feds could identify him from just his face: he'd never been arrested, so no mug shots existed. His driver's license and passport were forgeries; there were no documents that he knew of tying his real name, Grym, to any photograph of him. Part of the reason for him undertaking this assignment was because he was "clean." The other part had to do with trust. But no matter what, he had no desire to test his face with the authorities; he couldn't afford to get caught.

He reached the door to the toilet at the end of the car and stepped inside. He didn't want to take his eyes off the boy and the briefcase for too long, so he did everything quickly.

He locked the door. Kneeled. Reached into the garbage bin—a metal flap marked TRASH. He found the small key exactly where she'd left it: stuck beneath a piece of duct tape on the back of the stainless steel flap.

He now had absolute proof the briefcase belonged

to him, if it came to that. The key warmed in his hand. He slipped it into his pocket.

He left the foul-smelling restroom and returned to his seat.

The boy and the woman hadn't moved. Just as he'd hoped.

Everything in its own time. He sat down.

At that same moment, the boy stood and waved at an approaching conductor.

The conductor caught up to the boy, who then spoke in an animated way to the man. The conductor looked up at the overhead rack. The boy bent down and produced the briefcase.

More talk. The boy passed the briefcase to the conductor, who looked it over, thanked the boy, and moved on.

This was Grym's chance. He would stop the conductor, explain that the briefcase was his, and produce the key to confirm it.

But if the man made him open the bag, what then?

Kill a conductor?

The conductor walked by him holding the briefcase.

Grym told himself to do this now—get the briefcase, get off the train. But it was hours yet until

Toledo. Did he want the conductor to have all that time to think about any conflict with the boy's story? Did he want him making a radio call up the track to authorities at the next station?

He'd wait.

There was plenty of time.

5.

The train had been under way for the better part of two hours, Steel having long since turned the briefcase over to the conductor. Even so, he found that the case was all he could think about. It had wormed its way into his thoughts. In his mind's eye, he saw the woman arrive onto the train and place the briefcase in the overhead rack. He watched her sit down. He witnessed her leaving the train without it. He recalled his pursuit of her out onto the platform. Her refusal of the briefcase. Curiosity mixed with confusion, and, as always, his mind sought answers.

The conductor had been pleasant enough. He'd thanked Steel for his powers of observation, his honesty. But the mystery that now shrouded the briefcase tugged at a bored teenager who found himself stuck on a long train ride with little to do.

"There's plenty to do," his mother said. "You can practice your speech again. It counts as twenty-five percent of your overall score."

"Mom."

"I'm just suggesting."

"How 'bout I go see Cairo?" he asked.

"Maybe in a while. We need the conductor."

He didn't press it. If he challenged her too much, she'd deny him just for the sake of asserting her authority. He knew to wait it out and try again in a few minutes. Repetition won the game.

Farmland slipped past in a blur. Seeing the cows in the fields reminded Steel of his father and a car game they played called Hey, Cow!, where you rolled down a window and shouted "HEY, COW!" at the top of your lungs. You tried to pick out the first cow that would lift its head and look toward the car. It cracked up his father every time they played.

"When do you think we'll see Dad?" he asked his mother.

She did that thing where her face bunched all up: half anger, half frustration. He understood that he should *not* ask that question again.

Her cell phone rang. His mother was a long talker, and Steel once again saw a golden opportunity.

"Boys' room," he mouthed, as she listened to the caller.

She nodded and turned to face the window for privacy. Steel made for the aisle. As he reached the restroom door, he glanced back: his mother hadn't moved an inch. Her head remained turned toward the window. He saw his chance and took it, tripping the button that opened the door and making his way into the next car.

And the next.

By the third car, he'd caught up to a conductor whose name tag read CHARLIE. He was the same conductor who'd taken possession of the briefcase.

"Excuse me? Do you think it might be possible for me to see my dog?"

Charlie stole a look at his wristwatch. "Not supposed to, but . . . don't see why not," he said. Charlie had something of a potbelly, and warts under his eyes. He led Steel back, talking over his shoulder about baseball the whole time. A fan of the Chicago Cubs, he couldn't shut up about them.

As they drew nearer to the rear of the train he explained to Steel how he wasn't supposed to let anyone inside the baggage car. Steel wondered if he was supposed to tip him or something. His mother had given Steel twenty dollars, but it was two fives and a ten, and he thought five dollars was too much to tip a person.

Charlie's next subject was dogs. He'd had a dog when he was a kid, a neighborhood mutt that had made its home on a vacant lot up the street. Charlie's voice was deep as a lake. Steel caught bits and pieces of his randomly told story. Whenever Charlie looked back at him, peering over those rows of small, black warts, Steel nodded thoughtfully.

Unlocking the baggage car door, Charlie said, "Typically we only allow service dogs on our trains. You must be special."

"My dad died," Steel lied.

This had the desired effect.

"Couple weeks ago," Steel said, adding to his story.

"I'm so sorry, kid," Charlie said.

"Yeah, me too," Steel said, feeling bad to see Charlie look so sad.

Steel saw Cairo's crate and hurried down the car to it.

"Listen, kid," Charlie said in a softer voice than just a minute ago, "I got me some business to attend to." A pack of cigarettes showed through the chest pocket of his thin shirt. Steel thought that was probably the business being mentioned. "This door locks from the outside when it shuts, but you can let yourself out anytime. Stay as long as you like."

"Thanks. Actually, I can't stay very long," Steel said. "My mother thinks I'm bothering you. But I'd like to come back if I could."

"Anytime, kid. No problem. I'll let your mom know it's no problem. You just come and find me anytime."

"Actually, it might be better if my mother was left out of it. She'll think you're just being nice because of . . . you know. And that'll just make her sad all over again." He felt like a real twit for toying with Charlie this way, but adults were such suckers, he couldn't help himself.

"I'll tell you what—it'll be our little secret. 'Kay?"

"Okay. Thanks."

"Just leave when you want."

"Got it," Steel said, thanking the man again.

Charlie left. Steel heard the door click shut with authority. Locked.

Having been left alone for hours in a strange environment, Cairo reveled in Steel's attention. She seemed frightened by the rumbling and shaking of the car, so Steel coaxed her out of the crate and gave her a big hug. She shook and sneezed, and Steel laughed. She wagged her tail so hard she folded herself in half. Then she drilled her cold, wet nose in under Steel's chin and pushed him off balance. He fell back and caught himself with both hands.

That was when he saw it: the briefcase. It was sitting on a shelf marked LOST AND FOUND. There was no mistaking it.

Cairo continued to compete for Steel's attention, but it was a lost cause. Steel gently pushed her away as she wagged and danced around him.

"Not now, girl," he said. She launched into a nose patrol of the car.

The briefcase stared down at him. It had eyes and a voice that called out to him: *Open me. Solve the mystery.*

He fought to resist, but quickly returned Cairo to the crate and secured the door.

He checked from one end of the car to the other, just in case Charlie might be spying on him. His sense of guilt rose, but he ignored it.

He pulled the briefcase down from the shelf and placed it on the floor in front of him. Studying it thoughtfully, he walked once fully around it. Then he kneeled and touched it. The leather smelled like the inside of a shoe store. It felt smooth to the touch.

He spun it around. Cairo studied Steel from inside the crate as Steel in turn studied the briefcase.

"I'm just curious," he told her.

Oh sure, she returned with a look that was all brown eyes.

He grabbed hold of the case and tried the two latches. Locked.

He had expected this, and yet it fanned the flame of his curiosity. He spun the briefcase around a little more intensely. Picked it up: it felt as light as he remembered. Shook it. Something moved inside, but it couldn't have been more than a couple sheets of paper. He tried the latches again. Locked.

Steel was a problem solver. His teachers reacted to him in nearly the same way, year after year: impressed at first, wary of him as the year wore on. Afraid he might be smarter than they were—which was ridiculous; he was smart enough to know he wasn't smarter than anyone: he just had a photographic memory.

He felt up to the challenge of the briefcase. He'd heard about picking locks—seen it done in movies, but knew nothing about it.

He considered prying the latches open, but he'd only break them. And then what? It wasn't as if Charlie wouldn't figure out who'd broken them.

He flipped it around and upside down and

studied the hinges. Nothing available there besides breaking them as well.

Think!

He noticed the four small, metal feet. Half domes of stainless steel, they occupied the four corners, allowing the bag to stand level when placed down. He examined the four feet. He tested one, trying to turn it, but his fingers spun and it didn't move. He lacked a good grip.

He tried using a corner of his shirt, but it didn't help. He looked around for anything else—a pair of pliers would do just fine. He walked the length of the car but didn't see a toolbox or anything useful. Sitting down again with the briefcase, he spotted a small chunk of chewed rawhide inside Cairo's cage—the remains of a chewy bone. He pinched it between his fingers and tried to gain friction on one of the feet. But it was no use. Not one to give up once he put his mind to something, Steel tried another of the four feet.

This one broke free of the leather and turned. Excited by the victory, he quickly unscrewed it. The piece came off in his hand: a circle of stainless steel with a smooth-topped bolt through it.

He put his eye to the bolt hole in the bottom of the case. No wider than the diameter of a straw, it was nonetheless a perfect peephole. But with so little light inside the briefcase, he saw nothing but shifting gray shadows. Still . . . *there was something in there.*

He tried to loosen another foot: it too unscrewed.

"We're getting it, girl," he said to Cairo, who followed his every movement, shifting in the crate and cocking her head.

Now with two holes, he put his eye to the first and angled the case toward the light. A soft gray cone of light spread inside. He angled it in another direction. He saw a newspaper article, some papers, and what looked like a postcard. He tilted the briefcase, working the postcard to a spot where he could see it. Then he tipped the briefcase to let more light inside.

The card wasn't a card at all, but a photograph—a Polaroid, maybe. . . . He adjusted the briefcase a second time, and more light filtered in through the foot hole.

From beyond the door came the sound of men speaking.

Steel couldn't pull his eye away—he was so close, so curious. . . .

The voices grew louder. They were at the baggage-car door.

At that same instant the photograph shifted and came into better view. Steel gasped.

It showed a woman in front of a row of broken windows, her mouth covered with duct tape, her eyes wide in terror, her hair stringy and sweaty. Her face looked like a horrific mask of fright. Across the bottom, written in black marker was:

G23: 3-4

The sound of keys tinkled. The men were coming inside.

Steel pulled his eye away from the bottom of the briefcase, his mind reeling from the horrible image of the woman with her mouth taped.

Then, with the door rattling as if about to open, he scooped up the two stainless steel feet and looked for a place to hide.

6.

Grym shifted from heel to heel, waiting for the gasbag of a conductor to shut up long enough to open the door. Grym had nodded off and lost track of the boy. The moment he'd awakened he'd gone looking for the potbellied conductor who'd taken the briefcase from the boy. He'd found him, smelling of cigarette smoke, making conversation with a woman who was apparently lost. How a person got lost on a train was beyond Grym, but he patiently waited out the exchange and then reported his briefcase as missing, giving an exact description and even producing the key to prove his ownership.

From that point to this, the old man had done nothing but talk—mostly about the batting averages of the Chicago Cubs. Grym had no use for baseball. He was into NASCAR.

At last the conductor unlocked the door and pushed it open. Grym looked into a car lit by a pair of skylights and a long row of overhead light fixtures. The walls were floor-to-ceiling luggage racks and custom shelves, with a single aisle down the middle. Some of the luggage and boxes and bags had been strapped down. Others remained loose. The car smelled oily, but not unpleasant.

"Where'd you put it?" Grym asked rudely.

"It's down here." The conductor moved slowly. "Anybody here?" he shouted.

Charlie reached the shelf marked LOST AND FOUND. He rifled through a few of the items and said, "Dang!"

"What?"

"I could'a sworn . . ." He moved a few suitcases left and right, still searching. "This is where I *should* have put it, at any rate. Lost and found. Pretty obvious."

"You did or did not put it here?"

"Thought I did, or I wouldn't be looking, now would I?" Charlie clearly did not appreciate Grym's tone of voice. "Must have been moved by one of my colleagues . . . one of the other conductors."

"The boy . . . the boy you said turned it over to you." Grym tried to take the urgency from his voice. "Did you let him in here by any chance?"

"'Course not. Rules is rules. You think I'd leave a boy in here unattended?"

"You can tell me, Charlie."

"You got the wrong idea, sir," Charlie said. "Ain't no passengers allowed in the baggage car, and that includes yourself. We'd better get you out of here, for just that reason."

"You mind if I look around on my way out? It *is* my briefcase we're talking about."

"My guess is one of the other conductors might have moved it. I can check with them and get back to you. One thing's for certain: that briefcase ain't going nowhere, and neither are you. Neither am I, for that matter. We got plenty of time to find it, and get things back regular like."

Grym reached high up on a shelf. He moved more suitcases around and rose to his tiptoes. He bumped into the dog crate and stepped around it.

Cairo whimpered at his feet. Grym possessed no great love of dogs. "Shut up!" he said, giving the crate a good stiff kick.

"Time to go," Charlie said angrily, mustering as much authority as possible. Under his breath he mumbled, "No need to take it out on the dog."

Grym said sternly, "I want that briefcase and I want it now." He stormed out of the baggage car.

7.

Steel pushed Cairo aside and crawled forward toward the wire-mesh door. As he had been curled up in the back of the vinyl dog crate, the briefcase clutched tightly in his arms, his legs ached from cramping as he struggled out through the crate door and, with difficulty, came to standing.

As best he could, he returned the two metal feet to the bottom of the briefcase, but the second did not, and would not, screw in all the way. His mind raced. Could he tell his mother about the photo? Had he broken the law by looking at the briefcase's contents? What would the owner of the briefcase, the man with the conductor, do if he found out that Steel had been poking around his personal property? Would he tie him up and tape his mouth like the woman in the photo?

He considered returning the case to the shelf, and letting it be found. But that woman was in trouble—serious trouble—and how could he help her if he surrendered the briefcase? The police knew how to handle such things.

He determined to hide it. He searched out and found a spot behind a large suitcase. He slipped the briefcase between the suitcase and the wall, and stepped back to admire his work.

"It'll never work."

He jumped, barked out a cry, and felt a wave of heat prickle through him. A girl's voice from directly behind him. He spun around.

She was sitting on a crate, wearing a pair of shorts, running shoes, a white T-shirt, and a gray Nutrier High School Athletic Department sweatshirt. She had a long face with pink lips and inquisitive green eyes set off by a circle of black on the edge of the iris.

He tried to speak, but his voice got caught in his dry throat.

"They'll find it back there," she said.

"Where . . . the . . . heck . . . ?"

"I was hiding over there." She pointed over her shoulder without taking her eyes off Steel, as if she didn't trust him. "Kaileigh."

"Steel."

"What kind of name is that?" she said.

"The kind I'm stuck with," he said. "My real name is Steven."

"What's with the bag?"

"It's a long story."

"It's a long train ride."

"What's with hiding in the baggage car?" he asked.

"You might say I'm kind of a fugitive. But if you do say that—to *anyone*—then, believe me, I'm going to make you pay. I'm going to tell about you trying to open it—the case. About taking the feet off. What was all that about, anyway?"

"None of your business," he said.

"It is now."

"Do I know you?" he asked.

"That is *lame*," she said.

"I'm serious: you look familiar."

"First state, then regional. Not that I noticed you. I didn't. But I can read," she said, pointing to the science challenge logo on his sweatshirt.

"Are you serious? You were at the challenges?"

"I was *in* the challenges. I'm the balloon girl."

"No way."

"Way," she said.

"You won," he said.

"In my category. Sure. But I was up against mostly lame-os trying to reinvent the model airplane. Not the best idea."

"I watched you in the finals. You used a cell phone to make a balloon rise or fall. It was *way* cool."

"Microchip technology," she said. "Simple enough."

"So we're both heading to the nationals," he stated. His initial flash of fear subsided, and he felt more human.

"Duh. You might say that, yeah. Although, I'm kind of only sort of going. Right now, that is; as of this moment. In a way. Just not exactly sure how it's going to work out."

"You either are or you aren't going," he said. "It's an invitational."

"I'm going to Washington providing I make it."

"Are you *trying* to be mysterious, or what?"

"I'm not exactly supposed to be here. Technically."

"Technically, where are you supposed to be?" he asked.

"At home. It's a long story."

"It's a long train ride," he said back to her. She smiled, and to him it seemed like someone had turned up the lights.

She said, "Some dufus stole my balloon gear from school. My project was written up in our community paper. You know: 'Look! A girl can actually do science!' Right after that someone broke into the school and stole everything. Trouble is, it's a pretty simple technology—the cell phone places a call, and a chip in the balloon basically answers the phone. It warms when it turns on. The gas in the balloon warms—the balloon rises. Basic stuff. Easy to rip off once you see how simple it is. But the frequencies and powering the chips was complicated to pull off, and that was the only gear I had. Meaning I can't exactly compete without them. My parents"—she paused and looked at her feet—"they travel a lot. My mom got this trip all set up for me and Miss Kay—she's my nanny—governess," she said with a fake haughty accent. "—Whatever. And then when my stuff got stolen, Miss Kay called off the trip. But I still wanted to go, *of course*, because I'm convinced my stuff was stolen so that somebody else could win the nationals. Miss Kay and I don't exactly see eye to eye. But hey, the train tickets were already paid for. So's the hotel room. So I figured, why not?"

"But if the ticket's paid for, why are you back here?" he asked.

"Because we're coming into a stop. I have a seat. I

have a *sleeper*," she said. "But I'm thinking Miss Kay's going to try to get me off the train, and that's not right."

"You *ran away*?" he said loudly.

"My parents are *never* home, so you can't exactly say I ran away from them. Besides, there's no way Miss Kay's ever going to report me missing, or tell my parents, because it'll get her way fired. First she'll try to get me back, and I've got to avoid that. I want my project back. I want to compete."

"A sleeper? All to yourself? You gotta be rich."

"My parents. Yeah. Really rich." She looked at her toes again. "You?"

"No. Not so much. My father's a salesman."

"What's he sell?"

"I don't even know. Technology, though he never explains it."

"My dad's a private art dealer. He and my mom, they travel all the time. Did I mention that?"

"You may have," he said. "You ran away?" This time with great admiration.

"I'm sure Miss Kay is majorly pissed off at me by now. There is no way I can afford to get caught. I am like in serious trouble if she catches me."

"I won't say anything."

"So what's with the briefcase?"

"I've got to get back," he said. "My mother's going to freak any minute."

"The back of the crate," she said. "That was pretty good thinking."

"Thanks."

"Nice dog."

"Yeah," he said.

"So why not put the briefcase in the crate with the dog? They didn't see you when you were in there."

"Good point." He wondered why he hadn't thought of that.

He opened the crate and placed the briefcase in the back. With Cairo up near the wire door, and cream-colored plastic covering up the rest of the crate, the briefcase was basically impossible to see, even when looking through the gate.

"If I come back and it's missing . . ." he said.

"No worries. I'm a runaway, not a thief." She smiled, and again the train car felt different to him. "Cabin ninety-six," she said. "You could bring me food, if you think about it."

"I might just do that."

"Good, because I get kinda hungry."

"I thought you said you only hide when we're heading into a stop."

"Yeah, that's true. But I avoid cruising the train

as much as possible. I'm thinking it's not such a great idea to risk being seen, on account of Miss Kay could have put the word out. She's smarter than she looks. And the dining car—that's a pretty obvious place to look for people. We need to eat."

"Yeah, well I gotta take off," he said hesitantly.

"So take off."

On the way to the end of the baggage car, Steel tried to prepare himself for any questions Charlie might throw at him. Steel believed that saving the woman in the photo could excuse a few white lies. He'd sneaked a peek at the face of the man looking for him through one of the crate's ventilation slats. The guy looked pretty normal, but he could easily be the woman's kidnapper, or a murderer, or something like that. Lying to a guy like that would be no trouble at all.

He turned. "How long are you going to stay in here?" he asked.

"Just until we're under way again. I was lucky to sneak in here when they were loading."

"I'm going to give it to the cops at the next stop," he said. "The case."

"Toledo," she said.

"That's the one. Me and my mom are sharing a sleeper car from Toledo the rest of the way."

"So maybe we'll be in the same car or something."

"So . . . see you later, maybe."

"You're going to have to explain that case to me at some point."

"Promise," he said.

But for now he just wanted out of the baggage car. His mother had been right: he never should have come back here.

8.

The chartered jet touched down at Metcalf Field, eight miles outside downtown Toledo, Ohio, a city that Larson had never visited. He and Deputy Hampton reached the bottom of the jet's stairs, where a rental car awaited.

Larson's quick movements and the tightness of his voice were partially the result of something he and Hampton had seen on the Union Station security surveillance tapes they'd viewed during the flight: a young boy.

The woman on the platform had been approached by a boy. There had been words between them. The boy seemed to be trying to return a briefcase to her, but it couldn't be ruled out that he was some kind of courier. Larson couldn't afford to overlook any possibility.

"At least we're ahead of the train," Larson said, proud to have beaten its arrival. "We'll monitor the platform. Anyone matching our suspect, or the boy, gets grabbed. If possible, we'll board the train and root him out."

"TPD is meeting us there," said Hampton, who'd made a call to the Toledo Police Department from the plane.

"We'll squeeze the train like a tube of toothpaste. If our guy makes a run for it, TPD will collar him."

"We could have used a better look at the boy," Hampton said. "We don't have squat to go on."

"Agreed."

"And this time of year, summer break and all, there are going to be a *lot* of kids on that train."

"I know that."

"Just trying to cheer you up."

"You're doing a great job of it," Larson snapped sarcastically.

They had the boy's general size, but that was about it. The distance of the camera and the graininess of the tape had failed to provide a good look at him.

Larson said, "Top priority: we don't want a hostage situation. This has to be handled carefully."

"Grym has a reputation for being good with disguises," Hampton said.

"I know that," Larson said irritably. "If you're trying to tell me the odds are against us, I'm well aware of that." He didn't like reviewing what had already been discussed.

Larson's cell phone rang and he took the call, driving one-handed. A moment later he hung up and said to Hampton, "The woman from the platform may have reboarded the train."

"No way!"

"Our friend at Terminal Security apparently spotted her."

"Righteous."

"We keep an eye out for her, as well," Larson said.

"This is getting interesting," said Hampton.

9.

Needing a drink, Grym headed to the dining car in the center of the train. At one end of the car stood a service bar, where an African American woman with a deep, kind voice sold him a Diet Coke.

Following the trip to the baggage car, he'd taken the precaution of changing his looks. He didn't want the conductor picking him out of the crowd and complicating things. Better to blend in with the rest of the passengers. He could always remove the disguise if he wanted to be recognized. He'd also taken a seat in a different car. With the train under way, no one was going anywhere—he had time to find the boy and the briefcase.

His personal ID was more of a problem—he didn't carry a driver's license for his current face. But if pressed, he could return to the restroom and change himself back in a matter of minutes.

He had to complete this mission. The equipment had been sent ahead. By now it had been tested and was ready to be put into place. A simple story in the newspaper had put this plan into action. Reworking the technology to their favor had been his brother's idea. Time was of the essence: the lottery's jackpot had crossed the forty-million-dollar mark.

The plan at hand was going to make them rich, and they were going to make some very powerful friends in the process.

Halfway through his Diet Coke, Grym glanced out the window at the passing countryside and, in the reflection off the glass, spotted a man staring at him. He allowed the man a few seconds to look away—and he did—but Grym's concern lingered. Who was the guy, and why had he been staring?

A minute or two passed. Grym checked the reflection again. The man wasn't looking his way, so he took the opportunity to observe the stranger: the man had shaved earlier in the day, nicking his face; he dressed well and wore expensive Italian shoes, but they'd recently been resoled. The Italian shoes didn't fit with Grym's stereotype of a federal agent or cop, and this relieved him. Maybe the guy had just been looking *out* the window, same as Grym.

He reviewed his options if things got tricky: it was possible to jump from a moving train, though he had no desire to try it. There were few if any places to hide on the train. He was glad he'd had a look inside the baggage car, because, as it turned out, that would be a good place to hide. Aaron Grym could pick almost any lock in a matter of minutes. If he wanted in to the baggage car, it wouldn't be a problem.

One thing was certain: he wasn't going anywhere without that briefcase. Above all, he had to find the briefcase.

Once again he shifted focus on the glass, and instead of watching the farmland, he saw that the seat behind him was empty, the man gone. He turned his head and looked all around the car. Gone.

Grym felt relief. He must have been wrong. But he couldn't be absolutely sure.

10.

A few minutes ahead of Amtrak's scheduled arrival in Toledo, Larson stood on the platform with Hampton. Twelve special-operations officers from the Toledo Police Department—dressed in black and wearing body armor vests—were dispatched to take their positions, and quickly disappeared.

Their commanding officer, a colonel named Bridge Knightly, addressed Larson with a firm handshake and a face void of all expression. Two German shepherds, handled by armor-clad female police officers—the K-9 teams—occupied positions on the platform itself. The backs of the officers' black windbreakers were marked TPD SPECIAL OPS in bold yellow letters.

Larson explained to Knightly, "Hampton and I,

each with one of your K-9 teams, will conduct a search that will meet in the middle of the train. No passengers will be allowed to disembark during the search. You'll detain anyone leaving prior to the conclusion of the search. Sound okay?" He offered the man the description they had of Grym.

"That's all you've got?"

"Yeah."

"Good luck, pal."

"I know."

Knightly said gravely, "If your guy is dumb enough to try to run, my guys are going to stop him. Enough said."

Larson said, "We need him alive. We want him alive. He has information vital to national security."

Knightly said, "Then you'd better hope he doesn't run."

11.

"All passengers are asked to return to, and to remain in, their seats and compartments," a male voice calmly announced over the train's public-address system. "We're to undergo a random security check in the Toledo station that will last no more than ten minutes. This will not delay our schedule as long as we gain the full cooperation of *all* passengers. Thank you for your patience."

Discontent rippled through the car. Grym tensed and considered the situation. The police certainly had nothing matching his current disguise. His only real risk came if they demanded identification. He doubted authorities would ask for ID from each and every passenger; such an action would take far more than the ten minutes that had been mentioned.

But he also knew this was no random check.

They were looking for him.

Did they know he was on the train, or were they just guessing?

To leave his seat now was unthinkable. They'd be looking for that kind of reaction. So, with his heart pounding, he put his nose down into a magazine and waited it out.

He blamed the kid for this. He blamed the kid for everything.

12.

Steel and his mother had just transferred to the sleeper car when the announcement came over the public-address system. Their compartment, number ninety, was only a few doors down from Kaileigh's, he noted. This would be their home from Toledo to Washington. A conductor had been nice enough to allow them in a few minutes ahead of arrival into the station, but now with the announcement of a search, Steel was fretting.

The room was small and narrow, but brightly lit. An upper bunk folded out from the wall. The bench seats converted into a narrow bed at knee height. There was a lot of plastic and stainless steel: a sink, a mirror, a small closet with a chemical toilet.

Steel had assumed that the security announcement

meant they were after him. The man had made a big enough stink about the missing briefcase, and now they were going to search the train. But it wasn't here in their compartment—so what was the worst that could happen? Was hiding the briefcase the same as stealing?

This felt like the perfect opportunity to tell the authorities about the kidnapped woman—the horrific photo in the briefcase. He tried to build up the courage to tell someone, but in reality he was terrified. He'd never said more than hello to a policeman before. How was he supposed to start a conversation? "Excuse me, sir, but I found this briefcase, took it off the train, then gave it to a conductor, then found it again, and now I've hidden it."

"Why did you take it in the first place, young man?"

"Well, you see, I have a photographic memory, and I saw this woman . . . It's kind of a long story."

"So the conductor currently has the briefcase?"

"No, sir. Not exactly . . . I kind of . . . It's in the baggage car with my dog."

"Your dog?"

Speaking of his dog, Steel's mother had arranged for him to take Cairo for a potty walk during the Toledo stop. Now she was irritated by the announcement that they'd be delayed. If they didn't get the chance to walk the dog soon, then Cairo would use her crate as a bathroom—and that would be ugly.

"This is going to cut into our time in the station," she said.

Then, all of a sudden, Steel realized this stop had *nothing* to do with the case and everything to do with Kaileigh. Her nanny had reported her missing—plain and simple. For a moment he relaxed. Then he tensed again: what if he was wrong?

He asked his mom, "But I can still take her for a walk, right?"

He was thinking that the best place to be during this security check was *off* the train.

She didn't hear him. She checked her phone—*again*. He knew she was waiting for a call from his father. She'd hidden her concern well for the past ten days, but Steel knew his father should have called by now. Again, he wondered if his parents were having problems. Again, he pushed it aside.

"What about Cairo?" Steel asked again.

"If she hasn't gone by now it's a miracle."

"It's not like she's been eating or drinking," Steel said. "Remember Montana?"

His mother grinned. Of course she remembered Montana, she said. The family had dozens of great dog stories.

He looked out as the train pulled into the station. Lady police officers with dogs. He grew increasingly nervous. Either he or Kaileigh was going to get it. What would his mom say when she found out he hadn't told her about the baggage car? He'd be grounded for life. She might even withdraw him from the science challenge to punish him. How was he going to tell the cops with his mom around?

He caught his mom staring at her phone again.

"He'll call," Steel said.

She smirked. Her eyes grew glassy. "Your father?" she said. "I spoke to him when you were in the restroom. Didn't I tell you?"

She'd never been able to lie to him. For years he'd been able to see through her lame attempts.

"Oh yeah?" he said, trying to sound excited. "That's fantastic! Did you tell him where we were?"

"Of course!"

"Is he going to come to the challenge?" What a weird game to play, he thought.

"He's going to *try*. It's the best he can do."

"That's cool. If he tries, he'll make it," Steel said.

"Don't get your hopes up," she cautioned. She looked a little panicked. "He's terribly busy."

"It's okay, Mom."

All of a sudden it looked as if she might cry.

He'd totally crush her if he told the police in front of her. She would freak out. He thought maybe the best thing would be to wait until Washington.

13.

As Larson boarded the front of the train, he entered a world of confusion.

Passengers had not followed instructions. Some of the elderly travelers seemed to think they'd been ordered *off* the train. Other passengers crowded the aisles clutching their bags, waiting to get off. A line five people deep had formed in front of the restroom. Some people had headed to the dining car, only to find the concessions closed, and were now crowding the back of the car, trying to return to their seats.

Larson took one look at the confusion and knew immediately that ten minutes was not going to be enough. Worse, Amtrak was not going to *give* him more than ten minutes. He'd never meet up with Hampton in the middle of the train, given how slow this was going to go. It was a blown operation before it began.

Tempers flared. Questions were shouted at him. More announcements over the PA system were drowned out by chaos. No one seemed in any hurry to comply with requests. Anarchy.

Larson scanned the rows of seats, looking for a passenger that matched the description he'd been given. The size and urgency of the task struck him. The dogs clearly offered him the best chance at identifying and apprehending a suspect; trained to detect gunpowder, gun oil, and several chemicals used in explosives, he wanted to get a dog on his end of the train, past as many passengers as possible.

He radioed Hampton and told him to forget about the boy for now. Their primary suspect remained their top priority. He wanted all efforts made to find Grym.

Hampton reported that the conditions on the far end of the train were as difficult as on Larson's end. He said, "We're into this one on a wing and a prayer."

14.

At the moment that Hampton received the call from Larson, his hand rested on a door handle to the fourth sleeping berth in the train car. He and a K-9 team had searched the baggage car with only one minor distraction: the German shepherd had gone a little wild when passing a crated dog. The shepherd wasn't supposed to "alert" to other dogs, and her handler had disciplined her. It certainly hadn't been alerting to Grym, so Hampton moved on, having no idea of the presence of the briefcase in the back of the cage.

He swung open the door to the sleeping berth. He faced a woman and a boy—a kid about the same age and height as the boy seen on the platform in Chicago. He stepped out of the way, allowing the

German shepherd halfway inside the berth, her nose twitching.

"Sorry for the intrusion; just a routine inspection."

"Doesn't seem very routine," the mother said.

Following a quick glance at the mother, he tried to meet eyes with the boy, but the boy—reading a book—didn't look up.

"Thank you," Hampton said, still hoping to make contact with the boy.

With the clock ticking, he jotted down the number of the berth—along with the train car—into his notebook and moved on. Apprehending Grym was the primary assignment. No one wanted money going to terrorists.

Some boy and his briefcase would just have to wait.

15.

At the sight of the U.S. marshal and the K-9 team, Steel freaked. For a moment he thought his heart had stopped. The marshal, an African American, had shoulders as wide as the train car door. He had a kind face, though he wore a serious expression. From behind him came the German shepherd. She nosed her way into the room while Steel's mother made small talk.

He wanted to tell his mother to shut up, to stop delaying the man and let him get out of here. After experiencing a spike of heat up his spine as the man attempted to make eye contact, Steel kept his head down and didn't look up again.

He knows something . . . he thought.

Finally, after what seemed like forever, the man

thanked them—*thanked* them!—and closed the door.

"Well, that was painless," his mother said.

Steel felt drenched with sweat.

"Are you feeling okay, sweetheart? You've gone pale as a bedsheet."

"It's my stomach," he complained, despite feeling fine.

"It's the fumes from the train. Ever since we stopped, I can hardly breathe," she said.

Steel didn't smell much of anything. Maybe some disinfectant and a trace of kerosene, but that was hardly the cause of his current state.

"Okay, they've seen us. All present and accounted for," his mother said. "If you want to check on Cairo, you're free to do so."

"I . . . ah . . ." He had no desire to risk running into that guy again.

"Are you telling me you don't want to? Sweet boy, you must not feel well. Oh, poor thing. First you bother *endlessly* about seeing Cairo. Now I *let* you see her, and you're not sure you even want to."

"I do want to see her . . . but . . . I don't," he said, rubbing his stomach for effect.

"Which is it—because one of us has to take her out."

The thought of his mother seeing the briefcase at

the back of the dog crate provided a miraculous healing. "No! No! I'll do it," he said, jumping up. He hoped by now the marshal and the K-9 team had left the train car.

16.

U.S. Marshal Larson spotted yet another teenage boy—that made five in this car. Hampton had been right about the train being crowded with school-age kids. Larson was glad his focus now fell entirely on Grym. But he had a cop's instincts, and he couldn't help but keep an eye out for the briefcase, the kid, and the woman—everything he'd seen on the security tape. Trouble was, there were dozens of briefcases in the overhead racks, more than that many teenage boys, and *no time*. He disciplined himself to stay on track.

The police dog followed just behind Larson, and behind the dog, the dog's handler. They passed through the first car into the second, where Larson again met with a sea of expectant faces and much of the same confusion and questioning he'd faced in the first car. Twice he stopped and asked for a passenger's photo ID; both licenses had looked legit, and the passengers in question didn't look enough like Grym for Larson to make a fuss. A logjam of irritated passengers clogged the car. The trio eventually reached the third car, Larson checking his watch in desperation.

Larson spotted the man at the window seat right away: he was about halfway down the car, with a pair of eyes that intentionally avoided him. Larson signaled the dog handler, and she picked up on it. Larson walked past the suspect. The handler and the dog moved closer to the subject but stayed in front of him. They had him boxed in. The only way out was through the window; and beyond the window there were TPD police officers stationed.

The suspect sat next to a middle-aged woman with graying brown hair. The last thing Larson wanted was a hostage situation. His heart raced painfully in his chest as he considered how to handle this.

17.

Grym's insides twisted: the cop—or fed—wearing blue jeans and a blue blazer seemed to be looking right at him. What to do? All the windows were emergency glass; he could get out if he had to. But how far would he get?

They'd squeezed him: the fed on one side, the K-9 on the other. A federal agent with brains—just his luck.

Again he considered the breakaway window. But no: they were likely to have the train surrounded.

He ignored the fed, keeping an eye instead on the dog handler, and watching for any reaction from her.

Without looking, he felt the fed's attention on him.

"Excuse me, sir," the fed said. And there it was.

Dread surged through him. Not outright panic. Not yet. But a clear sense of dread. Grym turned his head slowly.

The fed wasn't looking at him—wasn't talking to him—but instead to a man in the seat directly behind him.

"Identification please," the fed asked.

Grym turned back around, his nerves quickly restored.

The fed continued questioning the passenger. Out of the corner of his eye, Grym saw the fed studying the man's wallet.

The fed said, "I'd like to speak with you a minute in private, please."

The dog growled as the man came out of his seat.

The passenger was frisked. A rumble passed through the car as he was discovered to be carrying a gun. "I have a permit for that," the passenger complained. "You're making a mistake."

The fed said, "Yeah? Well, it's mine to make. Follow me."

Grym smirked. He contained his impatience, wanting a look at the passenger but not wanting to show his own face. He waited a few seconds and, as the passenger was about to be led away, caught a look at the man.

His breath caught: it was the man from the dining car.

The man who'd been staring at him.

18.

Larson led the suspect to a more private area where the cars met. He spoke quietly.

"What's the FBI doing on this train?" Larson asked in a hoarse whisper, still holding the man's wallet.

"What's a U.S. marshal doing blowing my cover?" the man asked.

"Explain yourself. I ask for your driver's license and you hand me your federal credentials. The K-9 alerted on you—so I knew you were carrying a weapon. What was I supposed to do?"

The FBI man crowded Larson's space by putting his face into Larson's. "You were supposed to figure it out and leave me alone."

The man was working undercover, Larson realized.

The FBI man said, "Get your people off this train now. You are interfering with an active investigation."

Larson said, "You bear an uncanny resemblance to a terrorist suspect. I'm Fugitive Apprehension." He let this sink in. Fugitive Apprehension was among the most elite and respected units within the Justice Department; only a handful of agents were ever selected to serve on the task force.

"Your search of the train could interfere with a three-year investigation," the agent complained. "And don't ask me what I'm doing on this train, because I am *never* going to explain it. My SAC will talk to your SAC, and *he'll* never explain it. So forget about it."

"I'm not worried about your case. I'm worried about my suspect. If your case involves my suspect, tough luck. I'm taking my guy off this train."

"Actually, you're getting off the train. And you're doing it right now." He pulled out a cell phone.

"Can't do that," Larson said, grabbing for the man's wrist.

The man pulled away. "You're going to force me, I suppose? Trust me: you don't want me to make this call."

Larson said, "I have ten minutes to sweep this

train—five now, if I'm lucky—and that's what I'm going to do."

Engaged in the phone call, the FBI man explained his situation . . . listened . . . then glared at Larson with intense and angry eyes. He cupped the cell phone and said, "You got a name for this suspect?"

"Who's asking?"

"What's the name?"

"It's need to know," Larson said, "and you aren't on my need-to-know list. And your boss isn't either."

The FBI agent shoved his cell phone at Larson, who reluctantly accepted it.

"Larson," he announced himself.

The tense voice on the other end ordered Larson off the train.

"I'm running out of time here. I'm not leaving this train until Amtrak forces us off."

Five minutes later, Larson, Hampton, and the dog teams were back on the platform.

Larson reeled with anger. "This is wrong."

"Yes it is," Hampton agreed.

"If I hadn't pulled this guy out of the crowd," Larson explained, "I don't think he would have stopped us."

"Their case—whatever they're doing on this

train—it's gotta be our case. Right?" Hampton asked.

"Not necessarily. I would doubt it. Theirs was probably planned way ahead of time. Ours was last minute."

"So what's going on? What's next?"

The train started up and pulled away.

Larson said, "I make some calls of my own. But I'll tell you one thing: we're not done with this train. Not by a long shot."

Grym decided not to leave the train in Toledo, afraid authorities might catch him.

He knew better than to test his luck. He needed the briefcase; the briefcase was everything.

And a briefcase didn't just disappear out of a baggage car, no matter what the conductor had said. If the bag didn't turn up by Cleveland, it would be time for a little one-on-one chat with the boy. He'd carefully watched departing passengers in Toledo, and he hadn't seen the boy or the mother among them. They were still on the train.

A person had to eat. Grym would watch for them in the dining car.

He'd look for them everywhere. He wasn't in any great hurry. He knew not to force the matter. The boy would show himself.

D.C. was still a long way away.

20.

Natalie Shufman had no idea what the contact looked like. The whole idea of a dead drop was that she could leave the briefcase without ever meeting the contact. Likewise, she doubted the contact had any idea what *she* looked like—unless he'd already been on the train watching her at the time she'd made the drop, and that seemed possible, but unlikely.

She'd returned to the train after the awful conversation with her contact in the station, having come away from it with the sense that someone might hurt the boy. She knew better than to involve herself with these people, but it was much too late for that: she was in this knee deep. There was no quitting, no going back. But the boy . . . His only crime was trying to do a good deed. He didn't deserve any trouble.

But how to find him and warn him? Where was he? She'd searched the train top to bottom a number of times, walking from one end to the other with no sight of him. She might have passed his mother or father, for all she knew—but that was just the point: she didn't know. She had no clue what anyone looked like beyond the young man who had approached her on the platform.

Frustrated and angry at herself for not having handled the situation on the platform better, she kept looking, walking the entire length of the train a sixth time.

And then she saw him: only the back of a head, but she was pretty sure it was the same boy. A moment later, when he happened to glance over his shoulder, she knew she was right. But there was one slight problem: he recognized her as well.

He took off like lightning.

Natalie hurried to follow, one car to the next. But the boy was shorter—harder to see—and fast.

Gone.

She stopped at the end of a sleeper car and turned around.

He had to be in here someplace.

21.

Steel knocked on the compartment door.

"Who is it?" A girl's high voice. Kaileigh.

"It's me! Hurry up!"

She pulled back the privacy curtain on the compartment door, and he glimpsed her face. Then he heard the lock turn. She opened the door, and Steel pushed his way through.

"What the . . . ?" she said.

"A woman. Following me," he whispered.

"Why?"

"The briefcase."

"What is it with this briefcase, anyway?" She spoke a little too loudly.

Steel hushed her.

"Don't shush me," she complained. "This is my cabin!"

At that moment, with his eye to the edge of the privacy curtain, Steel saw the blur of the woman's profile as she passed by. He raised his hand to silence Kaileigh. The woman stopped, as if sensing him. Then she turned around, and he could see her clearly; it was the woman from the platform!

He released the curtain and spun around with his back to the compartment's wall. His face was ashen. He waited a long time before daring to take another look. The passageway was empty; the woman had moved on.

He looked around. "Whoa!" he said softly, admiring the oversize compartment. "You *must* be rich. You have this all to yourself? It's huge."

"It feels small to me."

"Small? You should see ours," he said.

"Did the cops question you?" she asked.

"My mom handled it. You should have seen her." He paused. "What about you? I thought for sure they'd get you. It was you they were after, right?"

"Not. They stopped here, and I told them my mother was on the train somewhere, and that she hadn't come back when the announcement had been made. The cop didn't seem too surprised. He was tight with it."

"Your nanny never boarded?"

"She's not my nanny." She paused. "No. Not that I know of, no," Kaileigh said. She sounded almost disappointed. "Maybe she went straight to Washington. Maybe she's waiting for me there."

"I thought you didn't want her to find you," he said.

"I don't."

"Doesn't sound like it."

"Shut up," she said. "You're safe now. You can go." She indicated the door.

"Please, could I maybe stay a little longer?" He raised his voice hopefully.

"I guess."

"Do you regret running away? Coming on the train?"

"No way!" she said. For a moment she sounded almost convincing.

"We need a plan," he said.

"What kind of plan?"

"One for you. One for me."

"I don't need your help," she complained.

"Sure you do. How are you going to get to the hotel?"

"Take a cab."

"You have money?"

"Of course I do. My parents left Miss Kay a whole

bunch of cash for groceries and stuff." She paused and looked away. "I kinda borrowed it."

"You stole her money?"

"It isn't her money. It's my parents' money. It was meant for me."

"This is not good."

"Trust me: it won't stop her. Slow her down a little, maybe. And there's no way she's going to tell my parents about it. She likes her job."

"Maybe not after this, she doesn't," Steel said.

"Good point." Kaileigh smiled. Then the smile faded and she turned to Steel intently. "So what's in the briefcase?"

He considered lying to her, or just not telling her at all, but it seemed to him they'd formed a team of sorts. "A photograph."

"A picture? So what's so important about a picture?"

"It's of a woman. She's tied up. She looks scared. Her mouth is taped. I think someone kidnapped her."

"What? Seriously? Then you have *got* to tell the police."

"I know."

"So why didn't you?"

"I don't know. I just didn't."

"Do you know how moronic that sounds?" she asked.

"You want to make it to the science challenge, right? Well, so do I. I'm going to be in a lot of trouble for taking that briefcase. What was I supposed to do, let the guy get the briefcase back? What if he's the kidnapper? I don't think so."

"You have *got* to tell someone," she repeated.

"It's better if I just get the briefcase to the cops and let them handle it. It's locked. There's no way they're going to think I saw what's inside."

"So do it."

"I'm going to."

"Like, when?"

"Soon. I've got to figure out how to do it so I don't get in trouble."

"Telling them what happened might help."

"Shut up," he said.

"What if that's why they boarded the train: your briefcase? Do you know how stupid you were not to tell them this?"

"A lady—the lady just chasing me out there—brought that briefcase on board. I saw her. Obviously she was supposed to leave it for someone—the guy in the baggage car, remember?"

"Of course I remember!"

"So who is he?" he asked. "I messed everything up. Now they're both on this train looking for *me*. What if they've paid off the conductors to help them? Who am I supposed to tell? How am I supposed to get the bag without them getting *me* first?"

"You were supposed to tell the cops when they were on board."

"A little late for that, don't you think?" he snapped at her.

"So, I could get it for you and turn it over to the cops," she proposed.

"No way."

"Way," she said.

"And when they ask who you are? When they ask to talk to your mother?"

She bit her lower lip. "Good point."

"There's no way this is going to happen before Washington. I can just leave it in the baggage room for someone to find, or turn it over to someone then, or something."

"Not if one of those two finds it first."

"I know," he said.

"It's complicated."

"It gets worse," he said.

"You've got two people searching the train for

you, and a briefcase you can't show to anyone, and it gets *worse?*" she asked.

"There was something written on the photo of the woman. The one tied up."

"A message?"

"Some kind of code maybe," Steel said. He squinted his eyes shut. "G, twenty-three, colon, three dash four. Handwritten. Black marker."

"Say it again," Kaileigh said. This time she wrote it out on an Amtrak notepad as Steel recited it.

G23: 3-4

She studied what she'd written. "Some kind of stadium seating or something? You know how the rows are always lettered and numbered?"

"I doubt it," he said.

"A meeting time: three to four o'clock on the twenty-third?"

"There's no month that starts with the letter G," he pointed out.

"A gate number," she said. "A serial number. Maybe some kind of code for a phone number. Maybe she's a patient in a research hospital. Maybe the woman in the photograph is G twenty-three."

"Get a life," he said.

"Have you Googled it?" she asked.

"Yeah," he snapped sarcastically. "I've spent a lot of time on my computer on this trip."

"I have a laptop with Wi-Fi," she said, pointing to the counter, where in fact a laptop was open and running.

"There's no Wi-Fi on a train," he said.

"It's a broadband wireless card. Very fast. Pretty cool."

"*Pretty* cool?" he questioned. He pushed past her, which required some contact—it wasn't all that big a compartment. He studied the laptop. Sure enough, it was connected to the Internet. "This is tight."

"Go ahead," she said.

He worked the keyboard, typing in the cryptic code he'd seen on the bottom of the photo. "I've got two entries for hypodermic needles," he said.

"See," she said. "Maybe it is some kind of test hospital."

"Some lighting companies. Something to do with hockey."

"Stadium seats!" she reminded him.

He flashed her a disapproving look.

He read down the list on Google. "Something to do with physics . . . A business journal . . . More lights. The National Weather Service Web site."

"So, nothing," she said.

"Yeah. Or more accurately, too much of everything."

"I like puzzles," she said.

"Yeah, me too."

"Sudoku?"

"I'm totally there," he said.

"So we need to solve this before we reach Washington," she said.

"If possible, though I don't see how. We need more data: who she is, why she's been tied up. Something more than we've got. And we need to avoid being caught," he pointed out.

"Tell your mother you're nervous about the competition and you don't feel good. Stay in your room. Or you can hang out here, if you want."

"Or maybe a little of both," he said, agreeing with her.

"Just don't get caught," she said.

"If I go missing or something, it's your job to get the briefcase to someone."

"You're not going missing."

"But if I"—he interrupted himself with an astonished pause—". . . do."

"What's up, Steel? You should see your face. You're pale as a ghost."

"My father," he mumbled. "He was supposed to take me on this trip. Not just my mom. Totally unlike him to miss this. But you should see my mother. . . . She said it was business—that something to do with business kept him from making it. But she's been acting real strange. Getting phone calls at all sorts of hours. Says she talks to him, but never when I'm around, never when *I* can talk to him, so how do I know she's telling the truth? What if he's gone missing?"

"More likely they've separated or something, and your mother isn't telling you about it. I have *so many* friends whose parents are separated or divorced, you wouldn't believe it. And the first thing they do is lie to the kids about what's going on. Every time." She paused. "Sorry about that," she said when she saw the effect it had on him. "Maybe that's not what happened with your dad at all."

"I've been thinking basically the same thing," he said, still considering her remark. "But the thing is, my mom would be a basket case, and she's keeping it together." He didn't like thinking about it.

"I'm sure you're right," she said. But she didn't sound convinced.

"I gotta go," he said.

22.

FRIDAY, MAY 30, ONE DAY BEFORE THE CHALLENGE

Platform eleven at Washington, D.C.'s Union Station was crowded with passengers moving tightly in a herd from the train to the station. Burdened by carry-on luggage and weary from days of travel, the passengers moved along quietly and with little regard to one another.

Steel and Judy Trapp were among the last to leave the train, partly because Steel—who had rarely left their sleeper compartment over the past twelve hours—took his time getting packed and ready. Also because they had to finalize arrangements to pick up Cairo once they were inside the terminal. Judy Trapp pestered her son with disapproving clicks of the tongue and exaggerated sighs, waiting for him to join her. "Hurry up, Steel!"

"I am hurrying," Steel said.

"You're usually the first out the door. What's going on?"

"I don't know," he said. Steel had spent most of his time preparing his description of the invention—to him the most difficult part of the science challenge. He would have to speak—all by himself—to a panel of five judges, explaining both the technology behind his project and its possible practical application. He wished his father were here to drill him—his father understood his project way better than his mother did—and nearly asked his mother what was going on with his dad's absence, but couldn't bring himself to raise the issue.

His mother had chosen to get as many images in front of him as possible, because of Steel's photographic memory. Steel had "invented" an electronic sniffer, combining some existing technologies into a roving, space age–looking device the size of a large dinner plate and shaped like a lentil. The interior electronics and mechanics were all his own invention, and his mother repeatedly quizzed him on its engineering and operation the way she believed the judging panel might.

Now, as they walked together through an empty train car, Steel struggled with a roller bag that belonged to his dad, bumping it against armrests and seats. Inside the bag was his science project protected by tightly packed clothes. He didn't like bumping it against anything. He caught sight out a window of the baggage trolley—a line of carts pulled by a small tractor—on which he spotted Cairo's crate. "Mom!" he said, pointing.

But by the time she looked, the baggage had passed, and she'd missed it. But she wouldn't admit to that. "Yes, dear," she said, pretending to have seen whatever it was.

As they rode an escalator up toward the terminal, Steel felt a rush of excitement: Washington, D.C., the National Science Challenge. For a moment he forgot the briefcase in the back of the crate—and the three people out there looking for him.

"Wait for me at the top," his mother instructed, correctly anticipating he'd want to hurry off to find Cairo.

"Yeah, yeah," he said.

As the escalator carried him to the top, it was like a screen had been pulled down, and with it a view of the terminal appeared. But it wasn't what Steel had expected. Instead he saw several policemen, a pair of tables, and black restrainers strung between posts, funneling passengers to a central checkpoint. Beyond the checkpoint were restaurants and shops—part train station, part mall.

Steel instinctively took a step backward and down a step, now alongside his mother on the escalator.

"Steel?" she said.

"Police," he said, wishing he hadn't.

"It's just security. They're only trying to keep us safe. Nothing wrong with that."

But to Steel there was plenty wrong. The checkpoint was attended by a pair of uniformed policemen, but it was the two guys in suits that bothered Steel—one of whom he recognized immediately as being the federal agent who had looked into their sleeping compartment and asked questions. That had been in Toledo, a day earlier. What was the same man doing here?

"What's the matter, Steel?" his mother asked as he slowed. "You're as white as a sheet. Don't be afraid of them. They're on our side."

Steel kept quiet, unable to get a word out. He looked around for Kaileigh and wondered if they were after her.

23.

Larson asked Hampton, "How about this one?"

"The woman looks familiar. Yeah, I spoke with them."

Larson watched the way the kid struggled with a roller bag. Kids could make even the simplest task look difficult. He had a stepdaughter who was in a hurry to grow up, and this boy and his clumsiness reminded him of her.

"Hello," Larson greeted the pair.

"Hi." A voice breaking between boy and man. Eyes that didn't look up, didn't make contact. A *tween*—stuck between his innocent past and a mysterious future.

"Good trip?" Larson asked. "Enjoy the train?"

"I guess," the boy said.

"Hello," the mother said.

Hampton asked for their tickets and ID. He added, "Tickets for both of you. ID only for you, ma'am. We don't need ID for the boy."

"Agent Hampton spoke to you earlier," Larson told the boy.

The mother nudged the boy, who finally looked up.

"To my mother. Yes, sir," the boy answered.

Spotting an identification tag on the suitcase, Larson asked him, "Are you Kyle?"

"No. He's my dad. He's . . ." He looked to the mother.

"He couldn't make the trip," the woman answered.

The woman's eyes suggested something was wrong. Larson didn't push it.

He described what they knew of Aaron Grym. "Did you happen to see such a man on the train?" Their answers were carried on their faces before they shook their heads.

The woman said how there had been a lot of men on the train matching that description. "We took a sleeper from Toledo," she explained, as if that excused them.

Larson assumed the suspect had been on that train

at some point. He could have jumped from the moving train, or left at an earlier station without detection.

The boy's face carried a troubled expression. Larson wondered if this stemmed from discussion of the dad—or something else.

"What's your name?" Larson asked the boy.

Larson hadn't asked any other kid for a name. Hearing the question put Hampton on alert; he stood taller and moved slightly to his right, putting himself between the terminal and the two.

"Steel," the boy answered. "Steven," he corrected.

"Steven, let me explain something: if a man matching this description said anything to you . . . if you observed . . . if you oversaw him doing something he wasn't supposed to, but are now afraid to say anything—"

"What exactly are you implying?" the mother asked, interrupting.

Steel shook his head.

Larson took a risk, deciding to push the boy; he fit the general look of the boy on the platform. "Tell me about the woman—the woman out on the platform."

"My son thought she'd left the briefcase on the train. He tried to return it to her, and she wouldn't accept it. We turned it over to the conductor," Judy answered. "That's all there is to it."

Larson and Hampton exchanged looks.

"Which conductor?" Hampton asked.

"I couldn't possibly tell you," the mother said. "I'm sorry."

With a nod from Larson, Hampton took off toward the train.

"Is Washington your final destination?" Larson asked Steel.

The boy nodded. "The National Science Challenge."

Larson looked over at the mother. "Where will you be staying while in town?"

"I don't see how that's any of your business," she said. "But it's the Grand Hyatt. My son and I are tired. It has been a long trip, and he has a great deal of preparation before the challenge. You are, what? Either FBI or Marshal Service. I'm not sure how to address you."

Larson cocked his head, impressed that she knew the difference. "Deputy United States Marshal Roland Larson."

"We'd like to get to our hotel now, if you don't object, Deputy United States Marshal Roland Larson."

"Please," he said, waving them through.

The boy glanced up at him sheepishly. It was this one glance, more than anything else, that told Larson he wasn't done with this boy. Guilt was written all over his face. They needed to talk.

24.

"I need a minute," Judy Trapp said to her son when passing the women's restroom. "Stay right here!"

"Actually, Mom, I'll be over with Cairo," Steel said, pointing to the oversize luggage area. Several signs hung over a long counter; one was for baggage storage, another for lost and found. The terminal-turned-mall hummed loudly as hordes of people milled about. Steel dragged his roller bag over to the counter. His mother, without objection, headed toward WOMEN.

As Steel approached the counter, a porter was just delivering some golf clubs and Cairo's carrier through a door to the right. Steel approached the carrier and stuck his fingers through the grate and was licked and nibbled by an affectionate Cairo. The crate didn't smell so good. Steel felt sorry for the dog.

As Cairo moved around the tight confines, Steel spotted the briefcase. The baggage handler headed back through the door. A steady stream of people paraded past him. Steel looked around, checking thoroughly for any sign of the man from the train. Not seeing him, he popped open the carrier door, shoved past a wagging Cairo, and grabbed hold of the briefcase. He quickly shut the cage door and lifted the briefcase onto the counter.

"Lost and found," he was about to tell the man behind the counter. But he caught himself, afraid the attendant might ask him all sorts of questions he couldn't answer. What if the man on the train checked the lost and found?

"May I help you?" the attendant asked.

"I'd like to check this, please."

"It's a ten dollar deposit," the man said, pointing out a rate sheet taped to the counter. "Ten bucks covers the first three days, two bucks a day thereafter."

Steel dug into his pocket for the bills and change he had collected from trips to the dining car over the course of the trip. He counted out a five, three ones, and enough change to reach ten dollars.

The attendant passed him a claim tag. "Don't lose

it, kid, or it'll cost you fifty to get it back. Not that I'd forget you. This here is my department, and I don't forget a face. But rules is rules."

Steel had no intention of ever going back for the briefcase. He would tell the cops about it, and that would be that. But he nodded as if this mattered to him, and he pocketed the claim tag to give to the police.

Relief flooded through him. He was free of the briefcase at last.

Or so he thought.

25.

"Where are the restrooms, please?" Steel asked the woman behind the hotel registration desk.

The woman pointed to a hallway across the Grand Hyatt's lobby, her face expressionless.

His mother bent down and whispered to him, "Can't you just hold it? We'll be in the room in a minute."

"If I could, I would. But I can't," he said. "Be right back."

He crossed the busy lobby, swollen by attendees of the science challenge and their families. There were dozens, maybe hundreds, of people going in every direction. But only one had stood out to Steel: Kaileigh. He'd spotted her furtively waving at him from the alcove marked RESTROOMS/TELEPHONES.

And he'd made up the excuse of needing the restroom.

"What's up?" he said, reaching her.

She wore a backpack and the same gray sweatshirt from the train. Her hair was a little mussed. She led him toward a bank of pay phones, out of sight of the registration desk. She grabbed his hand—for a second he thought she wanted to hold his hand—then uncurled his tense fingers and placed some change in his open palm.

"You've got to call the front desk," she said. "Make your voice as deep as you can. Tell them you're my father, Mr. Augustine. Mention my name. Say that you're running late but that you're dropping me off at the hotel front door and you'd like them to give me a key to the room. Tell them the credit card's on file—which it is—and that you'll be checking in later."

"This is crazy."

"You've got to do it for me."

"Why?" he asked.

She just stared at him. And somehow he knew she was right. "Okay," he said. She was already putting coins into the phone and dialing the number. "Ask for the front desk," she said.

"My voice isn't exactly deep," he reminded her.

"It's deeper than mine," she said.

A woman answered, and Steel asked for the front desk. He then dropped his chin and tried to sound older, repeating word for word exactly what she'd told him. This was the way his mind worked: he didn't need to hear something a second time.

To his surprise, the woman on the other end said, "We would be happy to accommodate Kaileigh, Mr. Augustine. My name's Angela and I'm currently on duty, but I'm just making note of it in the computer. She can talk to any of our hotel representatives."

"You've been most helpful," Steel croaked out. He hung up the phone and shrugged.

Kaileigh's eyes filled with delight and gratitude. For a moment he felt like celebrating with her, but then the worst thing happened.

He spotted the woman from the train: the woman who had left the briefcase behind. She was casing the lobby, clearly looking for something or someone.

He pulled Kaileigh with him to get a better look as the woman moved out of view. His mother finished up at the desk and was looking impatient. The woman spun around, still searching—*for him*, he imagined.

But then things got even worse: the woman

seemed to lock onto his mother. She moved toward her.

"Your turn to do me a favor," he said quickly and without reservation. "Stop that woman and turn her around. Ask directions or something. I've got to get to my mom before she does." He didn't wait for her answer. He bravely charged across the crowded lobby, putting people between him and the woman from the train, making a beeline for his mother.

Kaileigh came to his rescue, tugging on the woman's sleeve and turning her around. With the woman's back turned, Steel reached his mother—who was waiting with a bellman and a trolley filled with the dog carrier and their bags—grabbed her by the arm and moved her toward the elevators.

"Steel?" she said, surprised by his behavior.

"I'm kinda in a hurry, Mom." He couldn't immediately think of an excuse. "The stalls in the men's room . . . they were all occupied." He made a face of urgency.

"Oh, I see," she said, hurrying to keep up with him.

Steel quickly glanced over his shoulder to see Kaileigh still engaging the woman from the train. Kaileigh met eyes with him and, unseen by the woman, motioned for him to hurry. When the woman turned her head searchingly, Kaileigh tugged once more on her sleeve, winning her attention and buying Steel and his mother just enough time to reach the elevators without being seen.

The last thing he saw was Kaileigh breaking free of the woman and heading toward registration.

26.

Natalie Shufman hurried through the lobby for the street and fresh air. She'd been looking for the boy when a young girl had tugged on her sleeve and detained her. In that instant she'd spied a uniformed cop patrolling the lobby and, taking no chances, she'd left immediately.

She wondered if her own people had ways of tracking her. She hadn't checked in since the call she'd placed from Chicago's Union Station. They had to be wondering why. Trying to find the boy was not the smartest thing she'd ever done. But she felt an obligation to alert the boy of the trouble he was in.

The adrenaline settled out of her as she reached the sidewalk. She knew the boy's name—Steven

Trapp—from studying the science challenge program.

Now out on the street, she wasn't sure what to do. She'd broken the rules by coming to Washington. Her disobedience would carry consequences. She had to do this quickly. The group struck fast, and violently. She needed to get back to Chicago as soon as possible. She'd think of some excuse for her absence once she got back.

She summoned her courage and returned to the hotel. She headed to a house phone and was about to pick up the receiver when she spotted the curved eye of a security camera looking down onto her from the ceiling. Once the mother reported the call—and she was sure to do so—Security could trace it to a particular phone, the location of the phone to a particular security camera, the camera to her face. *Her face.*

She couldn't use the phone to warn them. She'd need to meet with the boy and the mother in person.

This wasn't going to be easy.

27.

Grym tapped his watch, wondering if the time could possibly be correct. He'd fallen asleep in the hotel room. He glanced outside at the dusk. But it wasn't dusk; it was dawn. He recalled leaving the train station and riding a city bus to within a few blocks of the Grand Hyatt. He recalled checking into a hotel just down the street from the Hyatt. He remembered the walk-through of the Hyatt and the adjoining convention center, staking out where the science challenge would take place, getting his bearings.

But he had lain down for a nap and fallen asleep—for the night. The science challenge's orientation was scheduled for nine a.m., less than two hours from now.

He had to use that time—when mother and son would be occupied with the orientation.

He needed that briefcase; he'd do anything to get it, including breaking and entering.

He quickly showered and changed clothes, the time ticking in his head. It was imperative that by Sunday morning he have the contents of that briefcase in hand. He concentrated on this one task, blotting out all else. There had to be a way.

28.

SATURDAY, MAY 31, OPENING DAY, THE CHALLENGE

Opening day of the science challenge competition always drew a large crowd: parents, corporate sponsors, and the press. The floor of the conference center had been turned into a kind of gymnasium, with bleachers on the sides. The contestants occupied chairs on a raised platform at one end of the rectangular floor. The judges occupied the very front row of the stage.

There were fifty students taking part in the challenge, one from each state, but many of the states had sent a reserve challenger as well—in case for any reason the chosen participant couldn't take part—so Steel's impression was that there were more like seventy kids onstage.

The event began with a demonstration. Last year's

winner took the floor. A robot went out and tried to pick up a glass. The glass shattered and the crowd let out a collective sigh of disappointment, only to be surprised when a second robot scurried out and cleaned up the mess.

The crowd applauded.

The introductions began. As each name was called, the student rose, walked to the front of the stage near a microphone, and shook hands with the judges, then returned to the seating area.

"It's going to be okay," he whispered to the boy sitting next to him, whose name tag read: JIMMY KRUEGER.

"Those are *TV cameras*," Jimmy croaked.

"Yeah," Steel said out of the corner of his mouth, "but who's going to watch the National Science Challenge besides our grandparents?"

Jimmy cracked a smile. He breathed for what sounded like the first time in several minutes. "I'm Jimmy," he said.

"Yeah. I'm Steven. But I'm called Steel." He paused as he watched the boy try to digest this. "It's a long story," he said.

"Montana," Jimmy said.

"Indiana," replied Steel.

The stage lights bore down on him from high

overhead, blinding him from seeing the audience. He discovered if he tipped his head slightly and raised his hand, he could see better. He saw Kaileigh in the bleachers, thinking what an injustice it was that her invention had been stolen and she wasn't sitting up here with him. There were a lot of people out there—most of them adults. His heart did a little dance in his chest.

To watch the audience was to see proud parents mouthing the name of their kid as he or she was introduced, to see the cameras in the far back of the room turning their single gray eyes in one direction or another, to see journalists taking notes.

There, two rows up the bleachers on the left, Steel spotted his mother. Her face begged him not to be mad for staring.

Steel nervously looked away and caught sight of West Virginia: a tall girl who wore thick glasses and had invented an automatic gear box for a mountain bike.

He shielded his eyes: was that who he thought it was?

"There's no way I'm ever going to win this thing," Jimmy said, discouraged.

Steel mumbled, "But we get a private tour of the Air and Space Museum and free passes to the Spy

Museum. You gotta admit that's kinda cool." He couldn't get over what he'd seen—whom he'd seen.

"I'd rather have a chance at winning. My father expects me to win. Yours?"

He forgot about Jimmy's question, and never answered. Because he panicked.

There, between the cameras at the back, stood the same two agents who had stopped him in Union Station. Federal agents.

29.

Larson and Hampton stood next to a camera tripod. Larson had no great love of the press, and he was uncomfortable standing near them. All of a sudden it felt to him as if the kid onstage had spotted him.

He signaled Hampton, and the two split up. Hampton took one set of bleachers, Larson the other. The plan was to work their way closer to the stage while searching for a man matching Grym's description.

But what followed surprised Larson: the moment he and Hampton passed halfway, a woman rose from her seat in the bleachers, moved down to the floor, and came right for him.

Larson recognized her as the boy's mother: Judy Trapp.

She stopped only inches from him, and though at first she made an effort to contain her voice, reason gave way to emotion, and with it her volume increased.

"How dare you *follow* us here! What is it you want? Do you know what kind of trouble you're causing? Steel needs to concentrate."

The judge onstage was continuing the introductions.

Judy headed back to her seat.

The judge rambled on, but neither Larson nor Judy Trapp was listening.

Larson's phone vibrated at his side. He glanced over and saw Hampton with a phone to his ear.

"Yeah?" Larson answered.

"I've just spotted the woman from the train. Fifth row, on the aisle."

Larson identified the woman. Same hairstyle. Maybe Hispanic. He couldn't be sure.

"Move in."

Steel couldn't breathe. It was like one of those nightmares that can't get any worse, and then it does. First his mother had gotten up from her seat—a major embarrassment. Then she'd approached the tall agent.

He felt cold all of a sudden. Cold, and sick to his stomach.

31.

Grym spent less than an hour at Shipping Central, a copy shop that offered everything from Internet access to FedEx. He color photocopied his Michigan driver's license—registered in the name of George Peters—on to a clear mailing label, and then tested attaching it to a blank, white luggage tag that cost all of a dollar. It looked good. Then he bought time on the computer-and-scanner combination and scanned his driver's license. All he needed was the right last name—the family name the room would be registered under. Working with Photoshop, he changed the name from George Peters to George Trapp, printed it out on a clear mailing label, and fixed the label to the luggage tag. A careful policeman would spot his handiwork in little time, but

Grym was betting that a hotel desk clerk would not scrutinize the license too closely. As it turned out, he was right.

He explained to the clerk at the Grand Hyatt that he'd arrived after his wife and son, and wanted to check in and then meet them at the science challenge. He made himself into an impatient father, eager not to miss his son's big moment.

He kept the license in his hand as he presented it; he did not pass it to the man behind the registration desk. The clerk glanced up at it, saw his picture, and confirmed the family name. "Welcome, Mr. Trapp." A moment later, Grym had a key card to room 1434.

He knocked twice. Waited. Knocked again. As he'd expected, mother and son were down in the convention center at the science challenge. Grym entered the small room. A short hallway led to a bathroom to his right and a closet to his left. The room held two queen-size beds, both unmade, an armoire that contained a TV, a desk and chair, and blackout drapes on the windows. He heard the thump of the dog's excited tail and spotted the beige plastic crate in the corner.

The open mouth of an unzipped duffel bag called to him from a bench at the foot of the bed. He spotted a roller bag, also open. He made quick work of searching the room for the briefcase.

It wasn't there.

He kept his work patient and calm: he didn't want them knowing he'd been here. Wondering if the kid had somehow gotten the briefcase open, he went about searching for the photograph—the all-important photograph. This search had to be done even more carefully, and he went about it methodically, leaving no spot untouched. He checked inside the dog cage: nothing.

He was about to give up when he checked the bedside drawer. He picked up the Gideon Bible and rifled through its pages.

A piece of paper fluttered out like a tiny moth. It settled on the carpet.

Grym bent over, retrieving it. He held it up to his face, pinched it between his thumb and index finger.

A receipt from Union Station. At the top it read: DAY STORAGE.

Grym turned it over, a smile widening across his tired face.

It was date-stamped the day before.

32.

Natalie Shufman had surprised the boy. A moment passed before she saw his mother talking to . . . *Could it be? But yes, it was!* . . . one of the agents from the train. The mother's gesturing was heated and intemperate.

Then she spotted the other agent from the checkpoint at the train station. He had his cell phone glued to his ear and was looking up at her.

Applause from the crowd.

If she was going to do this, it had to be now. Natalie stood and made her way toward the mother, two rows below.

If caught, then all was lost—not only for her but for the boy as well.

33.

Steel saw the woman from the train approaching his mother. All she could possibly bring was trouble.

He looked for some way off the stage.

Behind him there had to be exits.

He looked for the red glow of a backstage exit sign. *There!* Well off to the side and behind him. He saw not only an exit sign, but below it a crack of daylight from a partially open door.

Backlit and silhouetted in that shaft of light he saw . . .

For a moment he . . . floated, his head swooning. There was a man standing in the shadowy wedge of light that filtered through the barely open door. Steel couldn't make out any of the man's features. But he didn't need to.

The silhouetted shape took form.

It was his father.

Steel's legs went rubbery and weak. He reached for one of the chairs onstage and managed to keep his balance.

He took off running, dodging through the occupied chairs and heading straight for the exit, where the shape of a man exploded into the sunlight of the door opening and then vanished on the other side.

34.

Natalie Shufman reached the mother.

"You don't know me." She spoke with urgency, conveying the importance of her message. "And I don't know you or your son, but I've come a long way to tell you your boy is in danger."

The mother was too stunned to speak.

Natalie took advantage of the pause. "Leave town. Now. Forget the challenge. Trust me, you'll be glad you did."

"Who are you? Why are you doing this to me?" The mother sounded on the edge of tears.

"Your son—" But there was no time. Natalie met the mother's eyes, attempting to convey her sincerity. "Please, just leave here. Today. Right now. Get him home safely. I can't do anything more to help you."

With the agent nearing, Natalie abandoned the mother and headed toward the back.

She might have been pursued by the agent had the mother not cried out at the same moment.

"Steel!" A near scream.

Natalie glanced up onstage. The boy sprinted off the back of the stage and disappeared.

The agent gave up his pursuit, turned, and headed toward the stage.

"Steel!" the mother shouted out again.

35.

Larson moved the moment the mother called out. So did Hampton. A kid didn't run like that unless he was scared, and Larson wanted to know who, or what, had scared him so. He thought he had the answer: the woman in the crowd, the woman from the train platform—but why run from her?

He sprang up onto the stage.

The boy was gone.

A shaft of daylight penetrated from the right: the boy had gone *outside*.

He hurried off the back of the stage and headed in that same direction, out and into the blinding light; the boy had a twenty-second lead. Larson caught a glimpse of churning legs as the kid rounded the far corner at the end of the alley.

Larson blinked rapidly, trying to force his eyes to adjust to the light, but everything was a painful blur as he sprinted down the alley toward traffic. The place smelled of rotting garbage. Larson was a trained hunter. A hunter of humans. He was hunting the boy now, and was determined to catch him.

Hampton would know to stay with the mother.

No boy wanted to be caught. And boys were fast, and evasive, and clever.

He turned the corner and ran smack into a tidal wave of pedestrians.

36.

Steel caught sight of the man he believed to be his father. He didn't stop running, but in his heart of hearts he began to wonder exactly what he had seen and why he'd felt so compelled to pursue it.

If it was his father, why would he run away? Parents were dependable, but not always predictable. Hadn't his father promised to come to the challenge? So why had he hidden? And why was he afraid to be caught?

The street was packed with cars, both parked and moving, the air alive with the noise of engines, the squeal of brakes, and the occasional car horn. Music thumped and pulsed from within a shiny rig with spinning wheels. Steel leaped as he ran, too short to see very far ahead. People stepped out of his way, laughing.

He'd lost him.

His father was gone. Nowhere to be seen.

He bumped into a woman and got spun around.

And there was one of the agents, running toward him.

Determined he would not be caught, Steel spun and took off once again, this time the pursued instead of the pursuer. He skirted the flow of pedestrians by tightroping the curb, making his own lane. The great gray concrete wall of the hotel loomed to his left. He timed the next traffic light to cross without pause, dodging through gaps left by the crowd.

He stole a look back. No use: the agent was definitely closer, less than a half block behind. Steel dangerously recrossed the street, weaving through the slow traffic. Car horns sounded.

Another look back. The agent was stuck, unable to cross.

At the next corner, Steel ran left. But it was a mistake. The sidewalk here was less crowded, the going easier. The agent had crossed and was once again closing the distance.

"Stop!" the agent cried out.

Steel leaped between two parked cars and stole across the busy street amid another flurry of car horns.

He never slowed for a second.

37.

Worried not only about a young boy being out on the streets, but also concerned that he had been lured away from the science challenge, Larson had no intention of losing Steven Trapp.

The image that stuck with him was the boy racing across the stage toward the backstage exit.

Kids disappeared every day, baited and lured by dangerous individuals, never to be seen again. Parents warned their children about not speaking to strangers, not being tricked by questions about lost dogs or the chance to pet a kitty in an unfamiliar car, but kids didn't always listen.

Whatever had forced the boy off that stage had to have been a powerful force. He had to have known he'd get into trouble for leaving the challenge. What could account for that? If Larson could figure it out, maybe he'd have more to look for than just a small boy on crowded sidewalks.

He lost the kid for a second. When he appeared again he seemed ready to recross the street in traffic.

"Steel! Stop!" Larson called out. Then he jumped off the curb and into traffic himself. Tires yelped as a car skidded to a stop. Larson reached the other side untouched. But again he'd lost sight of the boy. He chased a flash of color to his left. In the confusion of cars and trucks and an army of pedestrians, he came to a stop, realizing he'd run right past the boy.

A doorway behind him.

Anger flooded him. He didn't like being tricked, especially by a kid. He was a professional man-hunter; a kid wasn't supposed to be able to fool him.

But kids liked games. And part of the secret to not being found was playing the right game at the right time. The more Larson thought about it, the more he disliked the idea of chasing kids. They could outsmart you.

The boy leaped from the doorway and started to run. Fast as lightning.

Larson briefly closed the distance, but it was like a bad dream: the faster he ran, the farther away the kid got.

Then the crowd swallowed the kid once again, and he was gone.

Any gap, any shadow might hide him. Larson slowed, taking care not to overlook a single hiding place. Valuable seconds ticked by. He reached a street corner. Looked both ways.

Nothing.

He'd lost him. A boy.

Worse, the boy was in the heart of the city now. Alone. A city not always nice to children.

The boy had smarts. He had guts.

Larson thought of the one person who might be able to predict his actions.

He turned and headed back to the hotel.

The mother would know.

38.

Grym saw himself as just like the wind: he was always there but you couldn't always see him.

He returned to Union Station in possession of the receipt he'd found in the boy's hotel room. The promise of success nibbled at him from the inside out, steadily chewing a hole in his anxious stomach. Arriving at the station—the mall—felt good; the air was cool and a welcome change from the outdoor humidity and heat that had built by midday.

He reached the day storage counter out of breath.

"I'd like to retrieve my things," he told the older man, a man with bent shoulders and a bulbous nose.

"Well, you've come to the right place," the attendant replied with a twinkle in his eye, taking the receipt from Grym. "Just a minute."

The old man wandered off down an aisle between stacks of steel shelving. It looked like a library for packages. He returned a minute later wearing a scowl on his creased face.

In his hand he held the briefcase.

Grym could nearly feel its handle in his hand. He'd never let it go. He'd never allow it out of his sight.

"I've got to ask you," the old man said, keeping the briefcase in hand, well below the counter, "where and how did you come by that receipt?"

"You . . . what . . . ?" Grym stuttered, not expecting a question like this.

"I'm good with faces, mister. Names?" He waved his free hand back and forth. "Ehh! But faces?" He poked his temple with a stubby index finger. "Clear as a bell." He paused. "And this here receipt was given to a particularly pleasant young man—thirteen, fourteen years old. He left us this briefcase and said he'd be back for it. And now you come along. And where I can see you've got yourself the receipt—ain't no questioning that!—I'd still like to know how you came by it."

Grym had no intention of answering the man. In another situation he would have jumped the counter and taken the briefcase forcibly. Who was this old man to question him?

"I gave you the receipt. Now give me the briefcase."

"The boy could have lost the receipt. Fallen out of his pocket. It's my job to get this item to the person it belongs to, not just the first person to show up with a receipt."

"I'd like to talk to your supervisor," Grym said.

"What do you think this is, some kind of corporation? You're looking at the supervisor, the desk clerk, and the sweeper-upper. There's only one other person works this desk 'sides me, and she fills in on Saturday mornings and when I ain't feeling well. So if you got a complaint, I'm listening."

Grym considered his options. He gained control of his runaway emotions, reached into his pocket, and brought out the fake ID he'd manufactured at the copy shop. He lowered his voice. "I'm the boy's father, George Trapp. It's my briefcase." He didn't allow the man's eyes to linger on the driver's license for too long—just long enough to see his face and read his name. He slipped it back into his pocket. "You'll find that the briefcase is very light, nearly empty"—he watched as the old man hefted the case—"and you'll notice when you shake it, it sounds like there's almost nothing inside, and that's because there aren't more than a few papers. But it *is* mine, and its contents are important to me. I could tell you what's inside and then show you, to prove that it's mine . . . but I'd have to kill you." It was an old joke, but one he'd never appreciated more than now. He won a slight smile from the old goat. "Why my son decided to turn this into a game, I have no idea. Probably to punish me for having to work while I'm here. But he's given me the receipt and I've come all the way down here, and he's competing in the National Science Challenge, and every minute I'm here debating this with you is a minute I'm missing some of the competition. So, if you don't mind . . ." He extended his hand.

The old man passed him the briefcase. "Why didn't you just say so in the first place?"

Grym couldn't stop the smile from overtaking his face. Just the feel of the case in his hand warmed him. "Thank you," he said softly, clutching the handle tightly.

39.

Steel slipped through a door without knowing where it led. He smelled fry oil as it opened, and he stepped into what turned out to be a deli. It wasn't terribly busy despite the noon hour. Maybe that was because of the scowl of the man with the rough complexion who stood behind the counter. He wore a red bandanna on his head like a pirate, and his mustache looked like a dish scrubber. He stood behind a tall glass case that offered hideous-looking meats. Small, handwritten signs had been stuck into the meat with toothpicks: tripe, sweetbreads, tongue, liver. The homemade sausage looked like something that had come out of the wrong end of Steel's dog, Cairo.

He asked for the restroom.

"Ain't no public toilet, kid," the grump growled.

"You gotta buy something 'f you want to use my can."

Steel didn't care about the toilet. He just wanted an excuse to go to the back of the store and find a way out. He thought going to the restroom might get him headed in the right direction.

He shot a look over his back, toward the street. Then another toward the back of the deli. How long until the federal guy came looking? He dug into his pocket for some money.

"Ah, forget it, kid. Go ahead," the man said, cocking his head toward the back. "No charge."

A moment later, Steel was in an alley that reeked of decaying meat, stray animals, and empty lives. It was a long, dark tunnel of brick and mortar, dented Dumpsters, and broken glass. Pieces of cardboard and sheets of gray newspaper, wet with rain, were fashioned into a small lean-to. A pair of bloodshot eyes peered out. A scabby hand raised to shield those eyes. Steel had never seen such a sight. For a moment he just stood and stared. Then a tail began drumming from somewhere inside, and a small snout with whiskers appeared from the gloom.

Steel thought of Cairo, and he couldn't wait to get back to the hotel to see her. He thought of his mother. His father. How he'd gotten here in the first place.

The dog growled. No, it was the homeless guy that growled. Steel took off, running right past the guy, the dog's tail thumping furiously with excitement.

And there ahead of him, at the end of the alley, came a silhouette much like the specter he'd seen backstage. His father? he wondered. Too small, he realized. The shadowy shape was backlit and difficult to make out. But as he ran toward it, it came more clearly into view.

Kaileigh. Waving, encouraging him to hurry.

40.

Kaileigh led him onto Fourteenth Street, to an upscale set of stores called The Shops at National Place. The White House was only a few blocks away.

"Do girls just know intuitively where there's shopping?" Steel asked.

"Shut up."

She found a small bookstore and they went inside, way in the back, where the books for young readers were kept. They were both out of breath, looking around to make sure no one had followed them.

"What was that about back there?" she gasped.

"Wouldn't I like to know," Steel said.

"What or who were you running from?"

"I wasn't at first," he said. He told her about seeing his father at the stage door and how he'd lost him once he got onto the streets. "Then I look back and I'm the one being chased. Talk about a nightmare."

"Yeah, I was in the audience. I saw you take off. But why run from this agent—whatever he is?" she asked.

"Are you kidding me?" he hissed. "This isn't about me. It's about the *briefcase*. Everyone wants that briefcase—that photo of the woman tied up."

"How do you know?"

"Okay, look. The agent . . . he mentioned the woman on the platform, a guy on the train . . . *the* guy on the train. And it's his briefcase. So what do you think it's about?"

"But chasing you?"

"I know! Explain that!"

"So what now?"

He considered everything that had happened, but couldn't think of what to say. "How about you? Any luck finding your project?"

Her shoulders fell forward in discouragement. "It's not listed in the program. I don't think it was entered."

"So it was just stolen."

"Looks that way."

"And you've come here for nothing?" he said.

"Not for nothing," she corrected. "I'm helping

you, aren't I? And I'm not done looking. Someone could try to enter it last minute. I'm not going anywhere."

"Your nanny?"

"She's not my nanny!" she objected.

"Governess, whatever."

"I have no idea," she said.

"So what do we do?" he asked.

"You could stay with me," she suggested.

"Yeah, right. Like that's going to happen."

"It was just an idea."

"It's a stupid idea. It's the same hotel as my mom, and besides, she's going to go crazy if I don't show up."

"But that guy's going to be waiting for you. You know he is. What do you think he wants to do, arrest you or something? Why would he chase you?"

"This really sucks," he said. "I've got to let my mom know I'm all right. I suppose I'm going to have to tell her about the briefcase."

He shoved his hands into his pockets and searched for the receipt.

"What's wrong?" she asked.

"I hid the stupid receipt in the hotel room. Otherwise we could go get the briefcase, and I could give it to that agent and be done with all of this."

"So go to your room and get it. Or I could do it for you," she said. "I can check out your room, maybe talk to your mom, maybe get the receipt, and make sure you're not in trouble."

"I've got to talk to her and explain this without those guys around."

"Let me help," she said again.

He eyed her up and down.

"How?" he said.

"I just told you."

"It's a lousy plan."

"What about your dog?"

"Cairo? What about her?"

She scrunched up her face into a smile. For a second he forgot all his problems.

"I've got an idea," she said.

41.

Larson stood with his back against the hotel room wall. Judy Trapp sat in the only chair, the one at the desk. Tears had streaked mascara down her cheeks, which were flushed red from crying.

"How much trouble is he in?"

"We don't know," Larson answered. "He's not in any trouble with us. But what you told me about this woman . . ."

"She threatened me. Told me we had to leave."

"But didn't say why," Larson said.

She blinked back some tears and shook her head.

"We'll find him."

"You don't know who you're dealing with. Steel is not just smart, Detective—"

"Marshal," Larson corrected.

"—he's . . . special. He's got a mind like a steel trap. Photographic memory. Reads at a college level. His invention for the science challenge . . ." she rambled, "they're usually half the parent, half the child. This was *all* Steel. And it's nothing short of brilliant. It'll get bought by the military or something. It can sniff out anything you give it a sample of. It's like a bloodhound. He's amazing. If he doesn't want to be found by you people—then you won't find him."

"We'll find him," Larson said. "He'll contact you. He may just come through that door."

"And the woman? The warning? What was that about?"

"She told you to leave."

"She said we were in danger."

"We believe she's the woman who was on the platform in Chicago. Maybe he wasn't supposed to see her face."

"Her face? Who are these people?" Her flushed cheeks went pale and her voice cracked as she squeaked out, "Do not tell me they're terrorists. . . ."

"We don't think so. They may have ties to certain questionable networks, but—"

"They *are* terrorists! OH MY GOD!" She came up out of her seat. "Are you trying to tell me without really having to tell me?"

"Mrs. Trapp! Please. Sit down. They are bad people, but not exactly terrorists. The man we're after . . . he and his brother are gang lords. We believe they have ties to certain international networks as well."

"Terrorists . . ." she muttered.

"Some of which are suspected terror cells, yes."

"Oh my God," she repeated.

"But that doesn't make them terrorists, only bad people."

"And why are you after this man?"

"I'm not permitted to say."

"It's something bad," she said, "or you wouldn't be after him."

"The point is getting your son back and keeping you both safe."

"I can't believe this," she mumbled.

"He might have fled from the auditorium in order to get away from her. We have men out looking for him. And the hope is he'll return here on his own."

The dog, lying at the woman's feet, thumped its tail, rose, and sniffed around Larson's ankles.

"She likes you," Judy Trapp said.

"Probably smells my dog on me," Larson explained. He looked at the dog, then back at Mrs. Trapp. "Has she been taken out lately?"

The mother looked up and met eyes with Larson. Hers were filled with expectancy.

"She must be . . . Oh, poor thing. I want to take her, but I also don't want to leave in case he calls or comes back."

"I can take her," Larson said.

"Would you mind?"

She handed Larson the leash. He was clipping it to the dog collar when he reconsidered. "No . . . no . . . It has to be you."

"I beg your pardon?" she said.

"It has to be you who walks the dog."

"But—"

"I need to get my partner in place."

"I'm not following you," she said.

Larson already had his cell phone in hand. "The dog," he said. "You said your son was bright."

"That doesn't begin to describe him."

"He's waiting for you to walk the dog. He knows you have to walk the dog, and he'll contact you then."

Judy Trapp's face filled with excitement. "That *does* sound like Steel, I have to admit."

"We have to handle this carefully. The police were notified by the organizers of the challenge. They are looking for Steel as well. And we want to get to him first."

42.

The afternoon traffic and pedestrians crowded the streets and sidewalks. Cars jammed the narrow street, filling all the parking spaces.

It was not the ideal environment in which to try to spot Steel while also keeping an eye on Judy Trapp and the dog. Worse for Larson was that hotel security had notified Washington's Metro Police that Steel, a minor, had fled the auditorium. The result was cops everywhere—one of whom, a detective, had been overheard asking a desk clerk to phone the Trapp room just as Judy—and Larson right behind her—walked past. Judy had glanced back at Larson, but he'd waved her on, not wanting to involve the local police just now.

Larson followed Judy at a distance, suspecting

that Steel was outside awaiting the necessity of walking the dog. He looked for a place along the street that Steel could use to see but not be seen. It seemed so simple, but looking up the street, Larson saw few possibilities.

Judy left the Hyatt behind, pulled by Cairo straining at her leash.

Larson hung well back, keeping his attention on Judy while appearing to be preoccupied with a phone call.

Despite the traffic and crowds, the street scene struck him as pretty. He thought Washington one of the more beautiful American cities; he attributed this mostly to the older architecture and the abundance of trees. They lined the street in full foliage.

Trees . . .

Kids . . .

He glanced ahead, searching for a good tree to hide in, and saw it immediately: an ash at the intersection of H and Tenth Streets. Judy would, by necessity, pass through that intersection. Larson couldn't see into the tree for all the foliage, but he didn't have to: he spotted a shadow cast down onto the sidewalk. Something—someone—was up in the tree.

He hurried ahead, stepped onto the shadow, and

said loudly enough to carry over the traffic, "I'll make you a deal, Steel. You, your mother, and I meet and talk this out." He paused as pedestrians passed. "I promise to work hard to keep you in the challenge." Again he waited for some people to walk past. "If the local cops or, heaven forbid, Homeland Security, get hold of you, you're out of the challenge and into a mess. I'm thinking that neither you nor your mother want that. So I'm going to take a chance now: I'm going to trust you. Don't blow this."

Larson's BlackBerry purred at his belt. He answered the call when he saw from the caller ID that it was Hampton. "Yeah?"

"Who the heck are you talking to? You're going to get carted away, you keep talking to that tree. What kind of freak are you?"

Larson hung up and looked around. He didn't see Hampton, but obviously his partner had a clear view of him.

He told the boy, who still wouldn't acknowledge him, "There's a coffee shop on the next corner. Don't come out of that tree until you see me reenter the hotel. Then head over to the coffee shop. If I'm not there at the top of the hour, then we try again exactly one hour after that. Got it? I'm not going to lead the cops to you. That's why we might have to wait. Your mother will be with me. I'm going to trust you, Steel, because I think I can. You break that trust, and it's the last chance I'm going to give you."

He hurried off toward Judy and the dog. Only as he crossed the street did he spot the dress shop's neon sign on the second floor of a brick building on the east side of Tenth. His money was on Hampton being upstairs in that dress shop, one eye on the street below.

His trust in the kid ran only so far. He called Hampton. "There's a kid going to climb down out of that tree I was talking to. Tail him and make sure he heads to the coffee shop on the next corner. If he doesn't, I've gotta know about it, and you can't lose him. Got it?"

"I'm on it."

"And, Hamp, whatever you do, don't let him see you. That kid has got some serious wheels."

43.

Grym contained his impatience. He stopped at a burrito joint that smelled like salty chips, and ate a taco salad, the unopened briefcase upright by his left leg. He kept an eye on the door and also outside the restaurant's plate-glass windows, alert for anyone watching him.

Only when he'd determined he'd not been followed, and was not being watched, did he finally lift the briefcase to the table. He slipped the key into the lock and turned.

It opened.

Just the feeling of the briefcase coming open filled him with a sense of success. Viewing its contents, a few sheets of paper and that all-important photograph, nearly overwhelmed him. He clicked the briefcase shut, checked the Metro map he had in his back pocket, and stood from the table.

He had an appointment to keep.

44.

Larson hoped Judy Trapp might stop walking the dog and return to the room. He grew impatient waiting for her to do so. She seemed to be stretching out the time, in hopes of finding her son. Larson didn't want to tell her he'd found the boy until they were alone and out of sight; he loitered about, making phone calls and pretending to be busy.

After another ten minutes, Judy Trapp got tired and turned around.

Back in the hotel room, he looked on as Judy fell to pieces. She had done an admirable job of keeping her worry contained; but now, sitting on the edge of a bed in a room with a federal agent, it poured out of her in the form of tears.

"I found him," he told her.

Her head snapped up in surprise.

"He was hiding in a tree. Same thing my little girl would do."

"But . . . where is he?"

Larson explained the deal he'd made with the boy. "My guy is keeping an eye on him. If he decides not to keep his end of the deal, we'll still know where to find him."

She stood and brushed the wrinkles out of her shirt. "What are we waiting for?"

"Top of the hour," Larson said. "Twenty-five minutes."

"Can't we go now? Early?"

"We're going to be followed by the local law. Questions will be asked. If we're going to do this, it's going to require some stealth."

"Tell me what to do. I'll do anything."

"I'm going to tell the others that you're taking twenty minutes in the gym to work out your stress. You'll go down there but will wait for me. We'll leave out the back."

She stared intently at him for longer than felt comfortable. He wanted to say something, to interrupt her penetrating glare, but couldn't think of how to put it.

At last she spoke. "Can I trust you, Marshal?"

"I would hope so, ma'am."

"I'm going to share with you something that can go no further than this room. No matter what your oaths and obligations. Do we understand each other?"

Larson shifted uncomfortably. "Those oaths and obligations are a little stricter than you might think, Mrs. Trapp."

"Judy," she interrupted. "And I know all about them, believe me."

"I can promise I'll do my best to keep whatever it is contained. That's probably all I can do."

"I'm not sure that's enough," she said in a dry whisper that raised the hair on the nape of his neck.

He debated what to do. Situations arose where a witness or a snitch provided you protected information, but Larson was sworn to tell his superiors if they asked.

"Okay," he said, "I won't repeat whatever it is to anyone unless I have your permission." He couldn't imagine what she might have to say, but she had certainly won his attention.

Judy Trapp screwed up her face into a pucker of determination and human will. The words spilled out of her. "My husband is with the FBI."

45.

Larson spotted a man who didn't belong. He stood at the end of the long hallway, guarding the elevator. It seemed possible the local police had involved hotel security, so he turned Judy around in the opposite direction and headed to the stairs.

"We need to talk about this," he told her at a brisk walk. "Your husband."

"I don't know much about his current assignment," she said. "Only that it's difficult, and it kept him from joining us. There was an accident. . . . A plane . . ."

"You know more than I do, and that needs to change."

He led her down the fire stairs to the floor below. Here, he inspected the hallway, grabbed her hand,

and led her out and down the hall, nearly at a run. He located a second set of fire stairs and took these to the mezzanine level. "It's a little bit cat and mouse right now."

"Anything to get me to Steel."

"That's the idea."

Now in the mezzanine, he studied the changing numbers above the elevators. "I'll bet they're looking for us." He sent Judy Trapp into the ladies' room. "Four minutes, exactly. Then out that far door under the exit sign. Turn right once you're outside. Walk casually. I'll catch up to you. Don't leave the sidewalk and don't turn any corners. Got it?"

"I'm good."

"Okay, then."

Judy Trapp pushed through the restroom door.

Larson marked the time.

Two men came out of the elevators: cops or security guards.

Larson allowed them to catch just a glimpse of him. Then he hurried off in the opposite direction from where Judy had gone.

They took the bait and followed.

Now at a fast walk—nearly a run he checked his watch: less than a minute to go.

The two men ran to close the distance before

Larson reached a door. One shouted, "Hey! Wait up!"

Larson slowed slightly, and at the last possible second before being caught, opened a meeting room marked for a gathering of pharmaceutical representatives.

The room held rows of tables with an aisle down the middle. A speaker stood behind a lectern, a PowerPoint presentation glowing on a screen behind him.

Larson hurried up the aisle. The speaker went right on talking.

He heard the two enter behind him, but by this point he was passing the raised stage. He pushed through an exit door and entered into a back hallway meant for servicing the various meeting rooms. He broke into a full run, moving left toward yet another exit sign.

He reached the brightness of the street, crossed through traffic, and ducked into a store. Judy Trapp would be somewhere on this street.

He watched through the store window for the two goons who'd been behind him. Only one showed up. They'd split up in the service corridor. This one had to decide between going left or right, and he picked right.

Larson gave him a few seconds to head off in the wrong direction.

Nothing so sweet.

46.

Grym arrived at the top of the impossibly long escalator leading from the Metro station, shielding his eyes from the intense sunlight. He took a moment to get his bearings, then found the street sign he was after, thinking that Washington was one of the most difficult cities to navigate. The briefcase felt ridiculously heavy given its lack of contents. The burden was more psychological than physical.

He trudged down the sidewalk, fighting for a chance to walk a straight line instead of stepping out of the way of people, increasingly upset at the lack of any system. In his world there was power and obedience, absolute order when required. Never mind that his soldiers were druggies and dropouts; they followed orders. His orders. Or his brother's. The world could do with a little less chaos and a lot more order.

He took a left, walked three blocks, and then a right. He stopped just long enough to drink in the beauty of the old cathedral. A recently constructed sign out front read: THE CHURCH OF HIGHER PURPOSE. It displayed the time of services and the television channel that carried a live broadcast.

Step by step, he climbed toward the church's massive door. Suddenly the briefcase felt heavier than ever.

47.

Steel sat at a table in the back of Starbucks, but only a few footsteps from the side door and freedom. He didn't recognize anyone, and wouldn't have trusted them even if he had. He kept an eye out for the woman from the platform and the man from the train. That was why he'd picked a table near the side door.

Kaileigh was his secret weapon. She'd been in another tree across the street when the agent had cut the deal with Steel. On her way down, she'd spotted the other agent watching Steel. If it hadn't been for her, Steel would have never known about that guy. Now she was sitting at an outside table near the side door, sipping an iced drink from a straw, keeping watch. They had a clear view of each other through the plate glass. If she removed the straw from the lid, then that was the signal that someone she recognized was coming. He'd be ready to run, and she'd be dumping her chair as a roadblock, the second he cleared the side door.

He knew he was in big trouble. He'd left the challenge without permission. The federal agent was trying to protect him from something. There was no way to undo that kind of stuff, but the idea of seeing his mom and of possibly remaining in the competition kept him in his chair.

Kaileigh had bought him an iced vanilla cream, and his stomach appreciated it. He waited. He wanted help finding his father. He wanted to give back the briefcase. He saw the chance to start all over, and he wanted that more than anything.

He kept watch, his eyes ticking between the shop's front door and the lid to Kaileigh's drink. The loud lady behind the counter seemed to be looking right at him. He overheard mention of the science challenge. For a few days, fourteen-year-olds in this town were rock stars: the *Washington Post* had run the headline "Teen Einsteins."

There were other kids in the coffee shop, all accompanied by at least one parent. He recognized some of them from the challenge. There were laptops open, cell phones in use.

Kaileigh pulled the straw from her drink. In the process the lid came off, and the drink spilled all over the place.

The front door opened. It was the same agent—tall, with a magazine-cover face. Steel tensed as the agent looked over at him.

About to flee out the side door, Steel spotted his mother. Suddenly he felt a lump in this throat. He wanted to run over to her, but for some reason he restrained himself. He didn't know how much trouble he was in, wasn't sure if he should tell her about having seen his father. Would she believe him, or think it was a lame excuse?

As the two reached his table, he finally stood and his mother hugged him. He actually hugged her back. She started crying, and he felt awful for having taken off.

"I'm fine, Mom," he reassured her.

They sat down. The man introduced himself as United States Deputy Marshal Larson. But they knew each other from the train station.

The marshal offered to get them both something. Steel ordered a hot chocolate with whipped cream and a cinnamon roll. His mother requested a latte with skim milk and shavings.

With Larson away from the table, Steel's mother

said, “I was so worried.” She stared at him through wet eyes. Then she reached over and touched the back of his hand. Her nails were chewed.

“I was all right, Mom.”

“You scared me.”

“I’m sorry.”

“Was it something I did?” she said. “Did I embarrass you or something?”

“Mom . . .”

“A woman whom Marshal Larson believes is the same woman from the train platform . . .”

Steel couldn’t keep the surprise off his face.

“She threatened me . . . us. Told us to leave.”

“It’s complicated,” Steel said. He looked over to make sure the marshal wasn’t listening in. “Dad was backstage at the challenge. He was watching me.”

Judy Trapp jumped like she’d grabbed on to an electric wire.

“That’s why I took off. But he took off, too. Why would he do that?”

“I . . . I don’t mean to be disrespectful, Steel,” his mother said, “but I think if your father were here, I would know about it. Don’t you?”

“Whatever,” Steel said. “I knew you wouldn’t believe me.”

“It’s not that.”

"Of course it is. You never believe me on stuff like that. Why do you think I took off? It was Dad."

Larson returned. He was a lot nicer than Steel had expected. Halfway through his hot chocolate, Steel found himself telling Larson about seeing the woman leave the briefcase on the train and some of what followed.

Larson looked at him intensely. "Your mother told me some of that. And while it's all important to us, it still doesn't explain their continuing interest in you."

Steel glanced out the window. Kaileigh was at her table, looking like she was about to come out of her skin. She clearly couldn't believe he was talking to the agent. Steel considered waving her inside, but feared he might upset her by doing so. If she wanted to come in, she'd come in.

"There's more, isn't there?" the marshal asked.

He looked up at his mother, then over at Marshal Larson. One promise he'd always kept with his parents was not lying to them. A few fibs, to be sure, but never a major lie.

He considered that Larson was basically a federal cop, and wondered if Larson would arrest him for having messed with the briefcase.

Larson apparently sensed his coming to grips with this. "My job," he said, "is to protect you and keep you out of trouble. I'm not here to punish you, Steel. I want to help."

"Sure you do," Steel said sarcastically.

"Steel!" his mother said sharply.

"At some point, you have to trust someone," the marshal said.

Steel thought about this. It was true: he hadn't trusted or believed anyone but Kaileigh lately, and it was wearing on him.

"You were curious," the man continued. "I would have been too."

His mother's reproachful look stung him.

"I went back to check on Cairo," Steel said. "Remember, Mom? That first day? And there was the briefcase. They'd put it in the lost and found." He recounted how temptation had won out and he'd explored the briefcase, resulting in one of the feet coming unscrewed. He left out anything about Kaileigh.

He felt the marshal's penetrating eyes on him. "You never got the briefcase open?"

"No!" Steel answered a little too hotly. "I promise. I never opened it."

"Which brings us to what you saw inside."

Steel made the mistake of meeting his mother's eyes.

"Steel?" she said curiously, "did you *see* something?"

"I told you: I never got it open."

"Something's scaring you, Steel," the marshal said. "And it has to be more than simply picking up that briefcase."

So Steel told him. He blurted it out. "There was this photograph . . . this lady . . . all tied up and stuff . . . and it really freaked me out because her mouth was taped and she looked . . . I don't know how to describe it . . . but it was for real . . . and I couldn't give it back . . . not if it meant they were going to do something bad to her . . . and why was the briefcase so important if they *weren't* going to hurt her?"

"You kept it," the marshal stated. His voice carried both surprise and something that bordered on relief. "You kept the briefcase. *That* is why they're after you. *That*," he said to Steel's mother, "is why the woman threatened you. Whatever's in that briefcase puts you both at risk."

Steel's mother and the federal agent stared at him. Their attention felt like the hot lights onstage at the challenge.

"I . . . ah . . ." he said.

"I didn't see any briefcase when we stopped you in Union Station," the marshal said.

"I . . . hid it. In Cairo's crate. The back of her crate."

His mother's face once again held both shock and disappointment.

He said, "I didn't know what else to do."

"It's okay, son. Where is it now? Where's the briefcase, Steel?"

"You know who that woman is, don't you?" Steel said accusingly. "What's with that? What's going on?"

"Steel! Please excuse him, officer. He's upset."

"They want the briefcase. Where's the briefcase, Steel?"

"Who says I still have it?"

"Steel! I won't have you talking like that. Answer the man."

"I checked it at the station."

The marshal exhaled audibly. "Do you have a ticket stub? A receipt?"

He nodded.

His mother's face knotted in concern.

Steel asked, "Please, can I still be in the challenge?"

48.

Grym's footfalls reverberated on the cold stone floor, the former cathedral's vaulted ceiling towering overhead. The Church of Higher Purpose occupied what had, for nearly two centuries, been a Catholic cathedral. Its ancient pews were now covered with deep-purple velvet cushions; stage lights were mounted high at the top of the stone columns; several scaffolding rigs held large television cameras. There was a public-address sound system suitable for a rock concert. Grym had been raised a Catholic, and he found the setting both soothing and confusing. It looked more like a television studio than a church.

When he reached the altar, out of habit he crossed himself. He then moved to the right. He passed through a door, down a more modern hallway that carried framed posters announcing stadium prayer events, and listing "The Right Reverend Jimmy Case" in bold letters. He heard the hum of computers. A man stepped into the hallway and greeted him with a false smile.

"Hello, sir! Welcome. These are actually private offices. There's a sign—" He paused as Grym walked right past him, gently connecting shoulders. "Sir? Excuse me!"

Grym turned. "Reverend Case is expecting me."

He reached the door marked OFFICE and walked in without knocking. There, he was greeted by a male secretary, equally surprised by the intrusion. As the secretary rose to intercept him, Grym held up a hand. "No visitors," he said. He let himself in through the only door available.

THE RIGHT REVEREND JIMMY CASE, read the name plaque at the edge of an enormous antique writing desk. On the walls hung dozens of framed photographs of Case with prominent politicians. Lots of forced smiles.

The Reverend occupied the chair behind the desk, looking as though he'd been saddled with an enormous burden. The two had never met, but Case had no question as to who this man was. Grym placed the briefcase on the edge of the desk, removed the photograph, and set it down in front of the television preacher.

“Sunday morning,” Grym said. He shut the case, turned, and walked to the door.

“Don’t hurt her,” the man’s quavering voice called out.

“That’s up to you,” Grym said, with his back turned toward the man. “Entirely up to you.”

49.

Larson pulled a veil of calm over his troubled face as he stood waiting and watching the boy ransack his own belongings.

"I swear," Steel said, "I put the ticket—the receipt, the claim tag—in the Bible. It was the one place I knew my mother wouldn't look."

Judy Trapp pursed her lips and blushed. "The room's been cleaned," she said. "Perhaps it fell out during the cleaning."

"Has anything else been disturbed?" Larson asked.

"What are you suggesting?" Judy Trapp said.

"Please. Look around. Other than a typical hotel cleaning, has anything changed?"

"It would be easier to answer that if it hadn't been cleaned," Judy said.

Mother and son took a moment to check their belongings.

Steel looked over at the agent. "Someone got in here? Is that what you're saying? Is that possible? Did that man take my claim check?"

"What man?" asked Deputy Marshal Larson.

50.

Natalie Shufman had spotted the contact from across the lobby an hour earlier. She hadn't recognized him—not his face, anyway. It was the way he walked. The way he moved. A determination about him. An *evil* about him that she'd come to identify. She'd traveled in a dark world for a long time now, but there was no getting used to it. Seeing this guy, she immediately feared for the boy: he'd come here to harm the boy, to question the boy, to kill the boy. She had little doubt about this.

She'd warned the mother too late. The mother hadn't listened. It was all going impossibly wrong. Because of her, a boy's life was now in jeopardy. She wouldn't be able to live with herself if anything happened to him. She had to do something.

She had to follow—to keep an eye on the boy.

To protect the boy at all costs.

51.

Steel waited to hear something about the briefcase. The agent had left to retrieve it—if possible. He stole a glance into his mother's troubled eyes. Her silence told him that she was furious. Whatever her initial concern for him had been, she now seemed to be considering how to punish him appropriately.

He hoped the marshal would return: he had much more to tell him. He wanted to figure out what was going on with his dad, for one thing.

"What about the challenge?" he asked, testing to see if she was ready to talk.

"How can you think about that *now*?" she asked, barely containing her anger.

He knew she was thinking of his dad. How could she not be?

"I'd still like to compete in the challenge, if I can," he said. He knew she'd want this as well; it all depended on how mad she was. "I was only trying to help. I thought she'd left her briefcase."

"And if you'd left it at that, we wouldn't be here." She started to look over at him, but her eyes never lifted off the floor. The words came painfully for her. "What you did was *wrong*. On the train, you said you were going to the bathroom while I was on the phone."

"I didn't actually *say* anything." This was a matter of honor for Steel—a longstanding promise. "And when I came back, I didn't tell you about finding the briefcase—I admit that—but I didn't lie about it either."

"Semantics."

"I didn't lie," he mumbled. Then he gathered his courage. "Are you and Dad getting a divorce?"

He appreciated the shock that registered on her face, because it said to him she'd never heard of such a thing—had never considered it. Either that, or she'd been expecting the question and was now acting.

"What?" she muttered.

"You and Dad."

"Divorce? Steel, I love your father. As far as I know, he loves me. Whatever gave you such an idea?"

"I don't know," he said. "Him missing the challenge, for one. And all those secret phone calls you're always having. And the way you don't talk about him, and you don't let me talk to him. I don't know."

"He's . . ." She screwed up her face while contemplating how to answer. "He's busy."

"Selling stuff. I'm sure."

"Don't give me that tone, young man. He's busy, and you're going to have to accept that the same way I do."

"You're lying to me," he said. "I can see it in your eyes, and don't try to tell me you're not. And if you can lie, then why are the rules different for me?"

She met his eyes. Then she glanced at the door, as if someone might come in. But the door was locked and bolted, so that was unlikely. She said, "Your father's not a salesman."

Steel's breath caught. He swallowed. "Okay . . ."

"His job is extremely dangerous, and it's secret in nature, and so . . . he thought it better to use what I guess you'd call a cover story—to protect *you*. Not him. His concern was always for you." She pushed some hair behind her ear, a nervous gesture he was well familiar with. "He's an FBI agent, Steel." She watched for his response, and although he felt as if he'd eaten ice cream too fast, he tried to give nothing away. He wanted more. "Undercover work. The highest security clearance. He reports to a man who reports to the director. That may not sound like much, but it's a big deal if you're in the FBI."

He wanted to discuss who had lied to whom. He wanted to explode in a rant and let her know just how upsetting it was to hear this. But it was also incredibly cool—his father an FBI agent—and it seemed the longer he kept his mouth shut, the more she talked. He knew this about her anyway: when his mother got nervous she could talk your ear off—although most of the time she said little of interest when in this state.

"He's been on a case," she continued. "I'm not supposed to know any of this, but I do. And with your memory . . . well . . . for once you've got to forget everything I'm about to tell you." She waited for him to nod. "He was working on a case involving a gang in the Chicago area with ties to very bad people. Someone must have found out about him, and they sabotaged his plane. The plane caught fire. If he wasn't such a good pilot . . ." She held herself together, but was clearly on the verge of losing it. "But he pulled off an emergency landing. No one could know he was alive after that. And he was worried about us. That's why he's missing the science challenge. He didn't want us on that train. We argued, and I misunderstood, and I put us on that train for all the wrong reasons. You knew I was upset, but I couldn't explain. It's a difficult and dangerous case he's on. It's had me rattled, and I'm sorry for that. Usually your father and I talk at least once a day, sometimes for hours. On this current assignment he rarely checks in, and when he does . . . when we've spoken . . . it's just that he doesn't want to lie to you, and he knew you'd have questions—"

"You think?"

"Don't get short with me, young man."

"Sorry."

"It's complicated," she said.

"You've lied to me for *years*. Both of you! I can't believe this."

"We knew you were getting old enough to talk to about it. I honestly think your dad intended to do that on this trip. And then he couldn't take the trip, and I know how upset he is about it."

"And you know nothing about whatever it is he's doing?" he asked skeptically.

"We established a long time ago that I'd know nothing about his work. The families of undercover agents . . . well . . . we're *all* at risk because of what he does. The more we know, the greater the risk. It's better this way. Difficult, but safer for all."

"But . . ." Steel struggled with what she was telling him. "Are you telling me . . . ?" He couldn't articulate all the thoughts and emotions swirling in his head and heart. It was like a loud rock song was generating a searing line of heat between his ears. He wanted to run. He felt cheated. *All this time*, he thought. "FBI?" he managed to croak out.

"I know it's a lot to take in," she said. "We'd always planned on telling you together. It's really his right to tell you, not mine. But given the circumstances . . ."

A knock on the door sent a jolt flooding through him. His mother collected herself—he hadn't noticed she had been crying through her explanation. She called out, "Just a minute!" toward the door, and she blew her nose and checked herself in the bathroom mirror. She then peered through the peephole and said, "It's Marshal Larson."

She opened the door. Larson, looking grave, stepped into the room and bolted the door behind him.

"It's gone," he said. "Someone . . . a man . . . claimed the briefcase an hour ago."

52.

SUNDAY, JUNE 1, THE CHALLENGE DAY 2

Sunday morning at nine o'clock, Steel waited in the challenge's "green room"—one of the conference center's smaller meeting rooms—with Kaileigh and about a dozen other kids. A TV in the corner displayed a closed-circuit feed of the stage. A college-age girl with a headset and a clipboard tried to keep them organized, but it was a bit like herding cats.

"So?" Kaileigh said impatiently, encouraging more explanation from Steel.

"So I told them about the picture," Steel said.

"No way!"

"I had to. That lady could be in real trouble."

"And?"

"And the guy flipped out," he said. "He took my mom and me to the Department of Justice, which is only the biggest building you've ever seen in your whole life, and this guy there, this tech head, had me describe the woman in the photograph while he drew it. Only, he didn't draw it; he used a computer."

"And how'd you do?" she asked.

"This is *me* we're talking about," Steel said. He reached into the back pocket of the khakis his mom had made him wear, and unfolded the color printout. "I have a photographic memory. Remember?" The photo that unfolded looked uncannily like the original, except that there was something sterile and mechanical about it: the woman in the chair, a row of broken windows behind her, her arms and legs taped to the chair.

"You did this?" she asked.

"A guy did it, I told you. I just described what I'd seen, and corrected him and stuff." He pointed to the handwritten code on the bottom of the computerized sketch. "This is what got the marshal—this guy Larson—all hyped up: the code. He said he was taking it somewhere to see if they could break it."

"Like, with spies and stuff?"

"Who knows? But once I told them that the photo was basically all I'd seen inside the briefcase, they let me rejoin the challenge. So here we are." He felt Kaileigh's disappointment. "Still no sign of your entry?"

"Why would anyone steal a balloon invention, if not to enter it in the science challenge? I just don't get it," she said.

"Maybe it'll still show up."

"It's a little late for that."

On the TV, yet another participant demonstrated his invention; it involved colored water and a membrane that filtered out all the color from the water.

"Pretty impressive," Steel muttered to himself.

"Don't worry: nobody's got an electronic sniffer like you do. You're going to do great."

"I doubt it," he said. "There's some pretty cool stuff."

"Best in the country," she reminded.

"Yours would have won. Controllable balloons? You kidding? I know they would have."

"Don't make fun of me."

"I'm not."

One of the other contestants, a boy who was also waiting to go on, grew restless. He milled about in front of the others, mumbling to himself pretty loudly. "Who cares about this stupid stuff?" he said. "What's the big deal about winning this thing, anyway?"

"Meltdown," Kaileigh whispered.

Steel nodded. He'd seen other kids collapse under the pressure at both the state and regional levels. Sometimes they just broke down in tears. Other times, like this, they started airing their complaints, as if everyone was supposed to care about their whining.

"Sit down!" one of the kids shouted. "I want to watch!"

"Down in front!" another kid yelled when Mr. Meltdown intentionally stepped in front of the television, provoking more anger from the crowd. "Move it, fatso! I want to see this entry!"

"You want to see?" Mr. Meltdown said, highly agitated. "You want to *see*!?" Now he was shouting. "I'll let you see!" He turned around and pressed the television's CHANNEL button, switching it from the closed-circuit view to regular TV.

On the screen, a preacher was giving a reading to an enormous congregation. "Today's scripture is from Genesis, twenty-three, verses three and four: 'And Abraham stood up from before his dead, and spake unto the sons of Heth, saying, I am a stranger and a sojourner with you: give me a possession of a burying place with you, that I may bury my dead out of my sight.'"

"Boo!" the kids jeered.

"Put it back to where it was," a high-pitched voice cried.

The image of the preacher dissolved into a still photograph—a color slide—of the preacher with a woman at his side. There was an address, a Web site, and a phone number printed below the picture. A voice came on explaining that it was time for the collection; he encouraged viewers to make contributions to keep their ministry spreading.

A narrator's voice said, *"We help those in their time of need. Our mission is the Christian word of God, and you can help us show others the way."*

"Oh . . . please," said Kaileigh, rolling her eyes.

Steel was about to make his own nasty remarks when the words caught in his throat. He coughed roughly.

Kaileigh turned. "Are you okay?" She reached up, prepared to slap his back. "I know the Heimlich."

Steel, now in a real coughing fit, shook his head and stabbed a finger at the screen: the preacher and the woman, with information printed beneath. Still unable to get a word out, he tapped at the printout Kaileigh was holding. Then he pointed to the television and the shot of the preacher and the woman.

"Oh . . . my . . . gosh!" said Kaileigh.

Steel recovered just as the screen changed to

a choir of women and men wearing red robes with gold collars. "That's her," he said. "The same woman."

Kaileigh studied the printout one more time. "I think you're right."

"I know I'm right," Steel said. "That's definitely the same woman who was tied up in the chair."

"What do we do?" she asked.

"No one will believe us," he said.

"They might."

"I'm not even sure I believe it," he said.

"It *did* look a lot like her."

There was an address on the screen where viewers could send their contributions. The city was Washington, D.C.

Steel coughed yet again. Something had stuck in his throat: fear.

"It's here. Washington," he said. "We could check it out. See if it's really her or whatever."

"What about the challenge?" she said.

"Trapp?" he said. "It's alphabetical. Are you kidding? I'm gonna be like, dead last. Always am."

"And your mom?"

"She parked me here knowing I'd be stuck in this room most of the day. We had this . . . fight. I think she's trying to reach my dad."

"Oh my gosh!" Kaileigh said. She rose out of her chair.

Steel thought this was a bit of an overreaction to his explanation. That is, until he saw that Kaileigh's face was now practically stuck to the television, which someone had turned back to the closed-circuit camera. Her finger was pointing, for Steel's sake, to an unpleasant-looking woman wandering in an aisle. She was short and wide and had a severe look to her.

"Miss Kay," she hissed.

It took Steel a moment to connect the name and the woman on the television to Kaileigh's governess.

"That's her?"

"Out of the way!" one of the kids shouted.

"Shut your trap!" Kaileigh hollered back. The protester sat down.

"She's looking for you," Steel said.

"Duh!" Kaileigh said.

On the screen, Miss Kay had found a woman with a badge—one of the challenge organizers—and was talking to her. The badge woman pointed.

"I've got to get out of here," Kaileigh said. "Now!"

Steel and Kaileigh moved toward an exit at the back of the room. Then Steel stopped and hurried over to a table where many of the inventions were displayed. He picked up his sniffer, a lentil-shaped orb the size of a large frying pan. It carried a retracting antenna and three wheels on the bottom. Steel pocketed the remote-control device.

"You're taking that with you?" Kaileigh said.

"After yours was stolen? You think I'm leaving it here?"

She shrugged.

Steel pushed open the door.

"How do we find the church?" Kaileigh asked.

"I memorized the phone number and the mailing address," Steel said.

Kaileigh looked at him as though he were a space alien. With his sniffer tucked under his arm, he pretty much fit the part.

"We're going to get in trouble for this," Kaileigh warned him.

"Yeah, I know." Steel smiled. "But we don't exactly have a choice."

53.

Steel and Kaileigh, having traveled by Metro, arrived at the church just as it was letting out. People streamed down the old stone steps. Pipe-organ music wafted over their heads.

"What now?" Kaileigh asked.

"We try to find the guy in the picture. The guy on TV."

The only person in robes they saw was a woman at the main door, shaking hands of parishioners as they left.

"She would be the assistant minister. Or whatever."

"That would be correct," Steel said.

"Then not through there." The woman minister had created a traffic jam at the main doors.

Kaileigh moved away from Steel and, looking down the sidewalk, motioned him toward her. She pointed to a side door also in use, but by far fewer people. "Choir entrance," she said. "Trust me. Been there, done that."

"So?"

"So that'll lead us into the back part of the church. As in offices. As in the minister's office."

"Okay."

Steel clutched his invention tightly to his side—it looked a little like a misshaped bowling ball—and they trudged down the sidewalk, intentionally taking their time to allow the choir to leave, not wanting to explain themselves to anyone.

Kaileigh bravely led the way up the narrow stone steps and through a black enamel door that carried a small brass plaque announcing: CHURCH OFFICES, and a smaller plaque added some time later below this one: PLEASE USE MAIN CHURCH ENTRANCE.

They tried to sidestep two women in a hurry to get out the door.

"May I help you?" the wider of the two inquired.

Kaileigh and Steel, both taken aback, froze with the question. Steel noticed the woman was carrying a folder. Kaileigh finally managed to squeak out, "No, thank you. We're just meeting someone."

The woman said nothing. She offered them a smile, held the door for them, and let it fall shut behind her. It clunked shut, the sound reverberating off the pale stone of the hallway.

"I've got a bad feeling about this," Steel said.

"You want to chicken out now?"

"I didn't say that."

"Then shut up. 'Cause I'm not exactly thrilled to be here either."

Faced with a choice of left or right, they inched down the hall to their left with great reservation. They were, in fact, barely moving at all.

"We keep up this pace," Steel said, "we'll be here all night."

"Yeah?" Kaileigh whispered. "Well, if you're in so much of a hurry"—she motioned ahead—"be my guest."

The sound of the organ came from ahead of them now. It drew them forward like a spell.

They passed several doors, all to their right. To their left towered tall, leaded windows of softly colored glass culminating in pointed peaks.

"May I help you?"

The low voice was a man's, and it came from an open door to their right. Both Kaileigh and Steel jumped, Steel nearly dropping FIDOE to the stone floor, but catching it somewhere around his knees, and fumbling it like a football.

He looked up into the face of the minister they'd seen on television: Reverend Jimmy. He wore a dark purple-and-black robe with bright red piping, and he stood very tall. His face was hollow, his eyes red and glassy with grief. He looked about a hundred years older than he had on television. Makeup was caked to his cheeks, caught on the slight stubble of beard where he'd missed himself shaving.

For a moment, Kaileigh and Steel just gawked.

Beyond the man, Steel saw the briefcase on the floor next to a large desk.

The briefcase . . .

"I'm sorry if I startled you," the Right Reverend Jimmy said. "This part of the church is—"

"My mother's in the choir," Kaileigh blurted out.

Steel found himself nodding along with her.

"Is that right? I'm sure I know her, then."

Steel's incredible memory saved him, for in that instant he recalled the name written on a song folder carried by one of the women. "Donna Pembroke."

The Right Reverend Jimmy looked puzzled and then . . . suspicious.

"Oh, Donna. Of course. . . . How can I help you children?" The Reverend didn't question whether they'd lied or not, and Steel appreciated that. It seemed that they all three knew, but the Reverend's voice was consistent and calm—nothing like Steel's father's voice when he smelled trouble.

"Actually," Steel said, "I have a message for your wife."

He didn't think it was possible for someone wearing so much makeup to go pale, but something drained out of the Reverend Jimmy like a plug had been pulled. He looked like a wax statue in the sun, all of a sudden.

"I'm afraid she's unavailable."

At that moment, Steel noticed a quotation stenciled on the wall. All this time trying to crack the code, and Steel hadn't made the connection. It seemed so stupid to have missed it. On the wall it read:

And God said, Let there be light, and there was light.
—Genesis 1:3

Steel blurted out: "G . . . for Genesis. Genesis, twenty-three. Verses three through four."

Kaileigh looked over at him as if he were crazy.

The Reverend's upper lip twitched, and his gray eyes narrowed under the weight of a crinkled brow. "Today's spiritual citation," he said, his voice like a dry wind. "What about it?"

"Your wife," Steel said boldly. He'd come this far.

"Anyway, I think she's your wife . . . the lady on TV with you. Today's citation: . . . Genesis, twenty-three. She's in danger."

"Who . . . are . . . you?" He took a step back into the safety of the doorway and the room behind him, like Steel and Kaileigh were some kind of devils. His eyes darted left and right down the hallway, expecting to see someone. He whispered harshly, "What . . . do . . . you . . . people . . . want? Using *children* as messengers . . . You tell them—"

"Who?" Steel interrupted. "Who did that to her? Is she okay?"

"We want to help," assured Kaileigh.

The Reverend Jimmy focused on the two children. "GET OUT!" he snapped at them. "If this is supposed to be some grotesque display of intimidation, you tell them—"

"Who?" Steel repeated. "Is she okay? Is she—?"

But before Steel could complete the question, the Right Reverend Jimmy Case had a heavy Bible in his hand, and the way he had picked it up—with both hands—it seemed he might use it to crush Steel's head.

Kaileigh tugged sharply on Steel's sleeve. But Steel needed little encouragement. The two of them took off running.

Reverend Jimmy called out loudly down the hall, "You tell them I did what they asked! You tell them to leave me alone! You tell them they promised!"

The man's rage and anger swirled inside Steel's head as Kaileigh reached the side door and threw it open to the heat and the snarl of traffic in the street.

Steel didn't forget a word of what he'd heard.

54.

With four of them in the hotel room—Steel, his mother, Kaileigh, and Marshal Larson—the space felt unusually small and confined. Five, if you counted Cairo, which Steel did.

"You shouldn't have done that," his mother scolded. "What were you thinking?"

"The code is a quote from the Bible," Steel said, directing this at Larson. "Genesis, twenty-three. Verses three through four."

"The minister," Kaileigh said.

"He *read* that verse—the code!—on television." Steel knew this was significant. "*That* is what this is all about: him reading the code like that."

Larson appeared agitated. He grabbed his cell phone, his eyes were darting about in controlled excitement. He moved away from the conversation, his voice low. But Steel overheard: "We've got a development on the Bible verse. . . ."

Steel realized they'd already known it was from the Bible. He wondered for how long. He wondered how much else they knew that they weren't telling.

Larson returned a moment later.

"You knew it was from the Bible," Steel said.

Judy Trapp shot her son a disapproving look, and he knew this had to do with the tone he'd used. But he wasn't thinking about being polite; he could only think of that poor woman tied up in the photo.

Steel said, "They used the preacher to get the code aired on TV. That way all sorts of people could hear it." He'd read how terrorists used broadcasts to wake up sleeper cells, to time their attacks. "Is something bad going to happen because of him reading that code?"

"We don't know," Larson said gently. "But that's certainly our concern, Steel, yes. The quote from Genesis could be what we call a trigger. It may have started something that we can't stop. Our people are working on it."

"But you said it was finances," Judy Trapp blurted out. "You said this gang was helping terrorists with financing."

"Seriously?" Steel asked excitedly. "Real terrorists? Are you *kidding* me?"

"I said," Larson corrected her, "that the gang is *believed* to be aiding terrorist organizations with their financing. We suspect that's the case, but lacking sufficient evidence—"

"So the code has something to do with money from—" Steel said.

"Don't interrupt!" Judy Trapp said, interrupting.

"Mom! I'm trying to help here."

"And you have helped, Steel," Larson said. "You too, young lady."

"I don't see how saying a code on TV helps give terrorists money," Kaileigh said.

Steel said, "The code must be a bank account or something like that. G, two, three, three, four." He asked Larson, "Am I close?"

"We don't know, Steel. We're working on it. No one knows. These things can take a long time to figure out, even with the best minds and the fastest computers."

"What's the letter G?" Kaileigh asked.

"What do you mean?" Steel asked.

"What number?" She began saying the alphabet aloud, "A . . . B . . . C . . ." and holding up a finger for each letter. She reached G and had seven fingers held up. "Seven-two-three-three-four," she said.

"It's not a phone number," Steel said.

"Too short for a bank account, right?" Kaileigh said.

"We're working on this," Larson repeated. "Give your mother and me a minute, would you, please?"

"You can go out onto the balcony," Judy Trapp told the kids.

"Can we take Cairo?" Steel asked.

"No, not on the balcony. And shut the door behind you, please."

The kids went outside and slid the heavy glass door shut.

"I'm sorry," Judy Trapp said.

"They've been a tremendous help. FBI agents—your husband's team, for all I know—are on their way to the church to speak with the minister. The NSA is working on decrypting the code. Transmissions like that—using the televised church service—are either used to secretly alert a lot of people at the same time, or as a means of separating power: no one person has all the information. But we're still in the dark. There's nothing more any of us can do here. As much as I'd like to say it's okay for your son to compete in the challenge, we feel at this point the best thing for all concerned is for you to return home. We'll fly you—privately—for the sake of your security. And our men will guard your house until this is over."

"That could be a long time. You just said so yourself."

"It's best. If these people believe Steel knows more than he actually does . . . it's not good for anyone. Our people are evaluating your long-term safety."

"Just what does that mean?" she said, clearly irritated.

"There are certain precautions—"

"We are *not* going into witness protection, if that's what you mean! We are *not* starting our lives all over, disconnecting from our families." She crossed her arms tightly. "I don't even want to *think* about that."

"Sometimes," Larson said cautiously, "that's the only choice. I'm not saying that's the case here. But we all want what's best, what's safest, for Steel. Your husband would, of course, be a part of any decision—"

"I don't want to hear anything more about it," she said. "We are not turning ourselves into nonpeople. This is not happening! All he did was try to return a briefcase to a woman who'd left it . . ." Her words trailed off and she held back tears. *Terrorists.* The thought of it turned her blood cold. "What's happened to us?" she muttered, her voice quavering.

The balcony door slid open.

Judy Trapp called out harshly, "We did not say you could come back in!"

But Steel raised his voice and covered most of what she said. "The Power Poker Pay Five!" he shouted into the room.

"It's a billboard across the street!" Kaileigh said, trying to point but getting her arm tangled in the gauze curtain.

"The lottery!" Steel said.

"This week's payout is . . ." Kaileigh untangled herself and leaned her head outside. She fought with the drapes again and faced Larson. "Forty-five million dollars. It's on an electric sign on the billboard."

"Maybe the terrorists plan to win the lottery," Steel said. "Five numbers. Lots of money."

"Don't be silly," Judy Trapp said. "They'd have to rig . . ." But she didn't complete her thought. Instead she found herself eye to eye with Larson. He looked troubled.

As Larson put the pieces together, he spoke quickly. "They used the church service to pass the code to a person who knew what it was for. They couldn't call him or e-mail him with the code, because those can be traced. They couldn't let anyone in the gang know who he was, because that kind of money is far too tempting. They had one loyal person they trusted, and they isolated him, waiting for this moment. His winning the lottery had to be totally unconnected to these people, so it couldn't be questioned once he won. By using the televised church service, there was no way anyone would know who he was or where he was or what he had in mind." He paused. "It's brilliant."

Then he recovered.

"I need to make a phone call," he said.

55.

"Freakin' kids," Larson said to Hampton, his front-seat passenger. "You understand that they beat the NSA—the freakin' NSA—to the solution?"

"I hear you," Hampton said, holding on for dear life. Larson was driving at a ridiculously high speed through the streets of Washington. He'd just run his third red light. "So I take it the reason you're driving so fast is on account we got something when we ran that number?"

"We asked the lottery people to access their accounts: Power Poker lotto number seven-two-three-three-four was purchased a few minutes past ten this morning: immediately after the church service went off the air. At a minimarket off Canal Street, southwest."

"Not the best part of town."

"No." Larson swung the car to the right, throwing Hampton into the door. Hampton double-checked his seat belt and locked the door.

"This is for tonight's drawing?"

"Correct."

"So they kidnap this preacher's wife and hold her until hubby broadcasts their code for them. Some guy they have planted over here—a sleeper agent—buys the lotto ticket, and surprise, he wins."

"He can give that money to whomever he chooses," Larson said. "And it's a pile of money."

"So the national lottery ends up financing terrorists," Hampton said.

"They must have loved the irony of that. How easy does that make things for them? We *hand* them the money they need." He yanked the wheel again, and again Hampton was thrown against the door.

"I'm driving on the way back," Hampton said.

56.

Two Big Gulp cups rolled around the convenience store's parking lot like kittens in a game of chase. Oversized handwritten posters in the store's floor-to-ceiling windows proclaimed:

50% OFF 64 OZ. SODA
GO NATIONALS!
USA NEWS ON SALE HERE!

The posters covered much of the glass so that you couldn't see into the store. But a weird, sterile light glowed from inside, and Larson caught himself squinting as he entered.

The woman behind the counter was a Big Gulp

herself. She had round, red cheeks, tightly set, pin-prick eyes, and puffy arms.

"Help you?" she said in what could pass for a baritone.

Larson displayed his credentials announcing he was a U.S. marshal. He enjoyed watching people's faces when he did this: sometimes eyes widened in awe, other times a look of panic spread across a face, putting Larson on alert. The woman behind the counter seemed unimpressed and even less interested.

"I need to ask you a few questions," he said.

"That's original," she said.

"About a lottery ticket."

"Wish I could tell you which one will win, but you're plum out of luck, fella. You gotta buy one and take your chances, same as everyone else."

Larson looked up at the ceiling. "I'd like to view your security tapes, if you don't mind. Ten-eighteen a.m., this morning. And I need your lotto receipts from between ten and eleven."

"What the heck?" she said, clearly puzzled.

"Work, that's what," he said, trying to downplay his interest. "All I really wanted to do when I got up this *Sunday* morning was put on a sport coat and go chasing lotto receipts in this charming neighborhood."

"Culmination of your dreams, I imagine," she said.

"Something like that."

"The security video's on a machine in the office." She jangled some keys in front of him. "I'd help, but I can't leave the register." She kept an eye on Hampton, who was roaming the chips aisle.

"He's with me," Larson said. "How do I work the equipment?"

"What do I know? Only way I know to make it work is to see it here," she said, pointing under the counter. Larson craned to see she had a view of four small TV monitors beneath the counter. "There ain't no TV back there," she said. "Probably some kind of switch got to be throwed, or something."

"I'll take a look." Larson eyed Hampton, who nodded. Hampton would keep an eye on the clerk while Larson visited the office.

He found an old dusty videocassette recorder sitting on top of a black metal file cabinet. It was running. He pressed STOP on the front and set it to REWIND, and then followed the cables up to the drop ceiling. It took him a moment to find the switch on the machine marked TV/TAPE, but once he did, he punched it and returned to the front of the store.

He and Hampton stood at the register and looked

down at the small TV screen. It alternated every five seconds between shots of the gas pumps and a view of the register. Larson noted the time in the upper corner as 12:25 p.m. He returned to the office and rewound the tape, shouting back and forth with Hampton until the time stamp read 10:15 a.m. Then together they waited and watched as a man entered the store and approached the register. He was a white guy, mid-twenties. Hard to get a good look at his face, but Larson thought the wizards at the FBI could enhance the shot and improve their chances. It took him five phone calls and a fax from the store owner to take custody of the videotape without a search warrant. How, or even if, it might help, he wasn't sure. All they had was the back of a head. But it was more than they'd had an hour earlier.

57.

Steel not only had an elephant's memory, he had the ears to go along with it: he could hear things clear across a room, which played to his benefit as his mother consulted Larson across the Grand Hyatt lobby. He'd also learned lipreading by muting the television while replaying movies he'd seen four and five times. He didn't make it public knowledge, but he could practically recite *High School Musical* from start to finish. The result was that he oversaw his mother's conversation with Larson, and overheard it as well.

Judy Trapp: Can't you just let him compete? I checked with the judges, and they have no problem taking him in the afternoon session.

Larson: We'd rather get you back home. Safer for everyone. The sooner the better.

Home? Steel thought. *Who was headed home?*

Larson: It's incredible that Steel and Kaileigh broke the code, and we were able to locate the lottery ticket bought for that number combination. But the trail has gone cold. We've failed to identify the individual in question. For your son's safety, it's important we move you as quickly as possible. There's no predicting these people. We'd rather err on the safe side.

Judy Trapp: But he's worked so hard. Come so far. His father . . .

Steel's brain deciphered her lips and he felt a chill race down his spine. *What about my father?*

Larson: The decision is made, I'm afraid. As soon as we round up Steel, we'll move you to transportation at the back of the hotel. I promise you'll be quite comfortable. The government views Steel as an important witness. You'll like the treatment, I think.

Judy Trapp: But the challenge . . .

Larson: I can't *make* you do this. It's voluntary protection. But the offer is there right now. I can't guarantee how long it will remain on the table.

Judy Trapp: Is that a threat, Marshal?

Larson: Not at all! Not intended in the least. I just know my bosses, that's all. An offer like this . . . the private plane, the full-protection team. They aren't made that often. It means we're taking your case seriously, and so should you.

Judy's eyes searched the room and found her son staring at her. For a moment there was a profound connection between them—one that Steel misunderstood, as it turned out.

He hurried to the ladies' room and kicked on the door. "It's me," he said. "We gotta get outta here!" He toed open the door a crack and shouted more loudly, "Kaileigh, it's me!" A woman gave him an inquisitive look as she left the room. Steel excused himself. "A friend of mine," he said. He felt like adding, "She's hiding from her Nazi nanny who's here because she stole a pile of cash and ran away from home." But the woman was gone, and Steel's toe was still holding the door open a crack when Kaileigh appeared.

"They're sending me home," Steel said.

"What?"

"I know. And there is *no way* I'm going home right now."

"You'd better not."

"So we gotta go."

"Where? How?"

"I saw the briefcase at the church."

"Yeah? So?" she said.

Steel patted FIDOE tucked under his arm. "So," he said echoing her, "someone dropped it there. At the church. Someone left that briefcase there, and I'm guessing I know who it was."

"The guy."

"Yes, the guy. And FIDOE can follow him," he said, rubbing his invention as if it were a genie. "FIDOE can detect four parts per million in a cubic inch of air. We can *do this*."

"What do you want to follow him for?" she asked. "We've been trying to get away from that guy."

"Once the preacher did as he was told, there were only two possibilities. One, the guy returns to the preacher's wife and lets her go. Or two, he returns to the preacher's wife and—"

"Kills her," Kaileigh said in a whisper. "She's served her purpose. Why keep her around as a witness?"

"But FIDOE can find her. I know it can." He glanced toward the busy lobby. "No matter what, if I stay around here I'm history. We're both history: your nanny is going to find you sooner or later."

"She's *not* my nanny."

"Are we going to talk about this, or are we going to do something?"

"Okay, but if FIDOE actually works, if we

actually find this guy, then we call the marshal. I am not going to end up like the preacher's wife."

"Agreed," Steel said. He pointed to an exit at the end of the hall. "We'd better hurry."

58.

On their second visit to the church, Steel and Kaileigh approached the stone structure's side door with a heightened sense of caution: the preacher knew their faces, and earlier he'd thrown them out. They weren't welcome. Adding to their fear was that Larson considered *all* these people dangerous, and that didn't rule out preachers.

Thankfully, there was something going on in the main hall: as the kids entered through the side door they heard organ music. A wedding rehearsal, maybe, for even through the thick door at the end of the hallway, it sounded as if there were a lot of people out there.

The hallway smelled of cleanser.

With FIDOE tucked under his arm, Steel kept to

the wall and moved cautiously toward the preacher's office, hoping beyond hope that Reverend Jimmy was presiding over the rehearsal. With each step the voices out in the main hall grew louder.

He and Kaileigh stood facing the office door, which hung open a crack. There was no telling if the preacher was in there. If he was, they would have to run.

Steel used the toe of his running shoe to nudge open the door. It squeaked on its hinges, and both he and Kaileigh winced with the sound and stepped back.

"What miracle is this?" said the preacher.

Kaileigh tugged on his sleeve.

"Wait!" Steel hissed. For his ear had heard an unnatural quality in the preacher's voice. Something wasn't right.

"Come on, let's go!" she begged in a whisper.

"That two people should find each other in the love and grace of God . . ." The preacher again.

Steel pushed the office door open farther. Empty desk chair. He glanced around inside: *no one!* The preacher's voice was coming from a speaker in the ceiling—there was a microphone in the main hall connected to this office so the preacher could monitor the church services.

The briefcase was right where Steel had seen it.

Kaileigh inched forward and stood with one foot in the office, the other in the hall. "This is *insane*."

"You want to help the woman in the photograph or not?"

"Of course I do!"

"Then stay there and act as guard. If the preacher shows up, you've got to stall him. You've got to buy me some time. FIDOE is incredibly accurate, but it's not exactly fast."

"Now you tell me!"

"Cool it. We're going to be fine. Just watch that door."

To Steel's amazement, Kaileigh cooperated. Through the overhead speaker, the minister reviewed the schedule of the ceremony. As long as he kept talking, as long as Steel heard him over the speaker, then all was well.

Steel set down his sniffing robot next to the briefcase and switched it on. When its lights blinked, flashing in several different colors, it looked like a miniature flying saucer. He moved the briefcase next to two small holes drilled through the plastic in the front of the contraption. These holes served as FIDOE's "nose." Steel held down two buttons until the red and green LEDs stopped flashing. Then he stepped away from the robot so its incredibly sensitive sensors didn't pick up his smell as well. It took approximately one minute for FIDOE's computer (a modified laptop) to process and record the scents. Until those lights started flashing again, Steel couldn't get near the device without risk of spoiling the sample.

"Someone's coming!" Kaileigh announced. She hurried into the office and then spun in a full circle in the center of the room.

Steel heard the hallway door thump. Then he heard something far worse: *nothing*. The overhead speaker carried the rumble of lots of people talking, but the preacher's voice was not among them.

He eyed FIDOE. The robot was on the left side of the big desk, partly hidden by the briefcase. There was no time to move it. He grabbed Kaileigh's hand and pulled her with him behind the desk. Now, down on all fours, he nudged the office chair out of the way, and he and Kaileigh balled themselves up under the desk. He pulled the chair back and tried to slow his breathing so he wouldn't give himself away. Kaileigh looked terrified. Steel held his finger up to his lips to indicate silence. She nodded.

The door hinges whined and the floor squeaked as someone walked across the room. Steel held his breath. Had the person spotted FIDOE? Was it the preacher?

Without the warning of more squeaking, a pair of black leather shoes appeared next to the desk chair. Another few inches and the left shoe would step on Kaileigh's fingers. Steel motioned for her to move her hand; she'd been too terrified to move at all, but now she snapped out of her spell and adjusted her hand.

"Where is that blasted thing?" said the preacher, talking to himself. He stepped forward, and the toe of his shoe landed right where Kaileigh's hand had been.

If he tries to sit down . . . Steel thought.

The preacher shuffled papers on the desk, moved the phone, and clunked down a paperweight.

"Aha! There you are!"

Kaileigh's face went white with fear.

Busted!

But then Steel heard the rustling of paper immediately followed by the sound of the preacher's footsteps moving away from the desk. A moment later, the preacher's voice came over the ceiling speaker.

"Sorry about that! Now, where were we?" the preacher asked his rehearsal group.

Steel and Kaileigh hurried from beneath the desk. Steel reached for FIDOE, seeing that the lights were blinking once again.

"It's programmed," he said.

"Let's get out of here!" Kaileigh whispered.

But Steel hesitated, drawn once again by the need to possess the briefcase. It was *his*, after all. He'd been the one who'd saved it in the first place. Furthermore, if FIDOE lost the scent, he might need to reprogram its sensors. He grabbed the case by its handle.

"Are you *nuts?*" Kaileigh said.

"Insurance," Steel said.

He tucked the robotic device under his arm. He and Kaileigh hurried out of the office—*without* first looking. Too excited after having been missed by the preacher, neither had checked out the hallway. They faced a bone-thin woman, quite old, who immediately reminded Steel of the woman tied up in the photograph. Her mother, perhaps.

"We . . . ahh . . ." Steel experienced a rare brain fart: he couldn't think.

"I'm a flower girl," Kaileigh blurted out. "I . . . left something in the car . . . and someone said we could get to the street from here."

Steel saw the woman eyeing the briefcase. "My father wanted me to put this in the trunk for him."

"First door on the right," the woman said. She eyed FIDOE tucked tightly under Steel's arm. "That's not some kind of music machine, I hope. We don't allow recorded music in our church. Organ and the human voice: those are God's angels."

"No, ma'am," Steel said. "It's a robot. I built it."

She gave Steel a look like he was the one from Mars, not FIDOE. "I've never seen a robot," she said.

"Maybe another time," Steel said, now being pulled past the woman by an anxious Kaileigh.

"First door on the right," Kaileigh said, repeating what she already knew.

The older woman turned and followed the kids with her eyes as they hurried toward the door. Perhaps she'd sensed Kaileigh's fear. Or maybe she disliked the idea of robots. Or maybe she'd seen through Steel's fibbing. But she kept her eye on them.

They practically ran down the hall and fled through the side door.

"I am *so* glad we're through with that!" Kaileigh

said, bending over and catching her breath out on the sidewalk.

"Through?" Steel said, checking FIDOE's blinking lights to make sure everything was running correctly. "We're just getting started."

59.

The boy's disappearance caused Larson another setback. Judy Trapp had gone hysterical when Steel melted into the hotel lobby and failed to return. There seemed to be several possibilities: Steel had been kidnapped by Grym or his gang; he'd taken off on his own, having sensed Larson's plan to send him home; or he'd thought he'd seen his father again and had pursued him. No matter what, his vanishing moved to the top of Larson's priorities: though he was in communication with FBI agents trying to close the door on the possibility of a lottery fraud, he wasn't directly a part of it.

Hoping to remain involved in the wider investigation, he sent Hampton back to the offices to work the phones and appeal to their superior to let them explore the broader crime. As marshals, their job was to protect the innocent or find the guilty; they weren't, by training or charter, investigators. If they were to remain a part of the hunt for Grym, Hampton was going to have to do some quick talking.

"We need to contact your husband," he told Judy Trapp, who'd returned to her hotel room in the hope that Steel might call. "Tell him that Steel may be following him."

"When he's on assignment, he calls me, not the other way around."

"There must be something you can do."

"I can call his handlers at the FBI. Is that what you want?"

"It's not my first choice," Larson admitted. He didn't need the FBI taking over *everything*. "But what if Steel was right about seeing your husband backstage at the challenge?"

"I doubt that."

"What if your husband is part of an FBI undercover team investigating this gang—this connection to terrorists? It's not impossible, you know? You told me yourself that he failed to make this trip with your son. What if that's because he was after the same person my partner and I are after? Believe me, it wouldn't be the first time two government agencies were working the same case without the other's knowledge. That would explain Steel's seeing him. And it also might explain why, if Steel had seen him, he couldn't make contact. If he's on the job, he can't reveal himself."

Judy Trapp looked up at Larson for the first time since their return to the room. Cairo thumped her tail furiously in her crate.

"The thing is . . ." Larson said, "if Steven is trying to catch up with his father, he could get himself *and your husband* into some real trouble, and your husband should know about that."

"Okay, I'll call."

"You can use my cell phone," Larson said. He answered her pained look. "My cell is secure. Hotel phones are not."

She nodded, accepted the phone, and dialed in a number. He hated tricking the woman—especially someone as torn apart as Judy Trapp. But the truth was, he needed to reach Judy's husband without her knowing it. No one was going to let him in on an undercover FBI operation.

But by using his phone to dial, she'd just given Larson the number to call. It was now in his phone's memory—a memory almost as good as Steel Trapp's.

60.

Steel placed FIDOE down onto the sidewalk outside the church and stepped back, pulling Kaileigh with him. The device spun several times to the left, and then repeated the procedure to the right.

"Is it broken?" Kaileigh said.

"It's searching for a matching scent," he explained. "It follows a pattern generator I developed by studying scent dogs. They usually work in ever-expanding circles—loops that take them wider and wider out. FIDOE does basically the same thing. But it comes across thousands of scents, of course, and it has to eliminate each one. I call this the progressive assessment stage—or PA. It can take anywhere from one to fifteen minutes to attach to the target scent. But once it locks on, it's able, ninety-eight percent of the time, to stay on the scent at a walking pace. Admittedly, I usually help it out by washing down the environment and putting out a single scent for it to follow: something strongly acidic, like lemon juice or garlic—"

"Are you telling me this is not field tested?"

"It is . . . in a way. But you might call this its first 'street test.'"

"There's a woman's *life* at stake."

"Have you got a better idea?" he asked.

"No! But you could have—" She didn't finish her thought. She was, instead, interrupted by the robot making a loud beeping sound. It spun sharply to the left, moved forward three feet, and stopped, only its green light blinking.

Steel stepped forward, kneeled beside the machine, and said, "Go!"

The robot took off down the sidewalk.

He turned to Kaileigh. "Voice recognition," he said proudly. "From here on out it will follow commands."

The kids walked behind the blinking machine.

"Are you telling me," Kaileigh said in astonishment, "that it's following the man who delivered the briefcase?"

"The probability is in the high nineties," he

answered. Again, he hurried to get close to FIDOE. "Stop!" he commanded.

The robot paused at the curb, facing across the street at a crosswalk.

Steel said, "We go this way." He bent down, picked up the robot, carried it across the street, and set it down on the other side. FIDOE spun around once, moved three feet forward, and paused, its green light unblinking.

"Go!" said Steel.

The two kids followed. Other pedestrians stepped out of the way of the strange machine beeping and blinking its way down the sidewalk. More than a few slowed and looked at FIDOE curiously. Steel followed proudly behind, Kaileigh at his side.

"Let me tell you something, Steel Trapp: you definitely would have won the challenge," said Kaileigh.

They stayed behind FIDOE for three more blocks. Twice the machine paused, spun in several loops, and then picked up the scent again. Kaileigh and Steel kept their heads down, following FIDOE and making sure it didn't run into any obstacles. Each time it reached a curb, Steel would pick it up and carry it across the intersection, starting it again on the other side. Sometimes it picked up the scent right away, and once it had to be restarted but soon found its way down the sidewalk again. Finally Kaileigh looked up.

"Uh-oh," she said.

Steel looked up, half expecting to see *the guy* or maybe the woman from the train. Instead he looked across the next intersection to see the black METRO sign: a subway stop.

"This is not good," Steel said.

"It's horrible," Kaileigh said. "If he used the Metro, FIDOE will never be able to follow."

"Never say never. There's a solution—"

"—to every problem," she said, completing his sentence for him. "Did your science teacher tell you that? Mine did." Steel nodded. "And I hated him for it," she continued. "Always making us think of ways around stuff, and giving you a worse grade if you couldn't come up with something."

"Yeah, but it's true: there are solutions to almost any—"

"But I don't want to *hear* it."

Steel understood computers and a good deal of math; but he didn't understand Kaileigh. Girls ran on different frequencies than boys.

Again, Steel carried FIDOE across the street. The robot led them to the impossibly long stairway that descended alongside the motorized escalators. The

Metro station was some eighty feet below the surface.

"I don't get it," Kaileigh said. "What do we do now?"

At that very moment, FIDOE emitted a pulsing tone that sounded like an alarm clock. A red light flashed.

"Oh no," Steel said, bending down to pick up his invention. "Its battery is running low." He cradled FIDOE in his arms like a baby. "If it loses power, or I have to turn it off, we'll have to reprogram it."

"Okay," she said, "so I was wrong about the briefcase. Now I see why we needed it."

"Slight problem," Steel said. "Minimum time for a full charge is three hours."

"The thing runs fifteen minutes on a three-hour charge? How practical is that?"

"I'm in beta: the weight to operational time ratio is critical. It was invented to win challenges, not hunt terrorists."

"We don't have three hours," she said, reminding him of the obvious. "Besides, fifteen more minutes of run time isn't going to help us much."

Steel racked his brain, pacing back and forth: FIDOE in one hand, the briefcase in the other. They were so close—on the path of the person who'd delivered the briefcase. He couldn't quit now.

People streamed by, stepping onto the escalator of the L'Enfant Plaza Metro station. One nice woman stopped to ask if they were lost.

Kaileigh answered, "Sort of, but we know where we are."

Steel smirked.

The woman looked at Kaileigh curiously and then continued on, mumbling to herself as she joined the escalator.

"Well, it was a good plan while it lasted," Kaileigh said. "And FIDOE worked in the field, which is more than most of us at the challenge could say about our inventions." She patted Steel on the shoulder. "We almost had him."

Steel turned away from her, unable to accept defeat. In doing so, he faced a dog walker who was coming down the sidewalk with five dogs on tight leashes. Finally, defeat gave way to inspiration. He turned around quickly, now facing Kaileigh, and said excitedly, "How stupid can we be?"

She looked at him, perplexed.

"Who needs FIDOE when we've got the real thing?"

61.

With the dead FIDOE tucked under his left arm, and the briefcase in the other, Steel climbed the hotel fire stairs to a door marked fourteen and peered through the small, safety glass window into the hallway. The long, dimly lit corridor stretched ahead of him, lined with a million doors. It was currently empty, but he waited patiently. He would know any second now if his plan had worked.

62.

On the lobby level, Kaileigh (who had pulled her hair into a ponytail in an attempt to change her looks) approached the front desk, all the while alert for the marshal, Miss Kay, or anyone else showing an interest in her. Forced to wait in line behind a sweating businessman, she stepped forward to hide herself among his luggage. The lobby hummed with conversation, and there were people everywhere; it felt to her as if *everyone* were staring at her, from the bellman to the concierge to a little old lady dressed all in pink. She wanted to shrivel up and hide.

Challenge contestants and their parents paraded past, some looking nervous, a few in tears. The process of elimination had begun. She ached for

Steel, who had given up all of that and now had so little to show for it.

Then, disaster: the dreaded Miss Kay. She entered the lobby from the elevator area—she'd probably been up in the room, waiting to surprise Kaileigh and drag her, kicking and screaming, back to suburban Chicago. But what to do? Kaileigh cowered, digging herself deeper behind the sweating man. He turned and looked down on her, his face florid, a sheen of perspiration clinging to his upper lip like a shelf of ice. He didn't smell so great either; he'd doused himself with cologne trying to disguise his true odor, and the combination was horrid.

The man moved forward in line. He was called to the registration desk. Kaileigh felt exposed. She missed the woman waving at her from behind the counter.

"Excuse me, miss?" the desk clerk called out.

At that moment, whether it was the clerk raising her voice, or just plain blind luck, Miss Kay looked over in that direction. She spotted Kaileigh immediately.

Kaileigh hurried to the counter, though most of her attention remained on Miss Kay, steadily approaching—working her way through the crowd.

"KAILEIGH!" Miss Kay called out.

"I think that woman—" said the desk clerk.

"Never mind her!" squawked Kaileigh. "This is for room 1434." She laid an envelope down on the counter. "It's *very important*—"

"Kaileigh Augustine, don't you turn your back on me!" Miss Kay yelled at about one hundred decibels.

"—that you tell Mrs. Trapp this has to do with her son. Please! It's of the utmost importance." She didn't wait for an answer. There was no time.

Miss Kay got tangled up with someone who thought she was cutting in line. Since Miss Kay rarely did anything outside the world of decorum, it was beyond her not to stop and explain herself. In that interim—that pause of a few precious seconds—Kaileigh made eye contact with the desk clerk, asserting her instructions, and then took off at a run.

"WAIT!" Miss Kay shouted, now raising her voice so that everyone in the lobby heard. "SOMEONE STOP THAT CHILD!"

It is a universe designed against children, Kaileigh thought, as not just one, but many, adults tried to grab on to her. Thankfully, she was about three times faster than any adult would ever be, so not one of them laid their hands on her. She cut left, considered the ladies' room, but decided it was the worst possible choice—a dead-end trap.

EXIT, read the red sign pointing to the door. Next

to the two elevators—elevators she didn't know existed—another sign: TO GARAGE PARKING.

She took the stairs. She'd meet up with Steel at the rendezvous. In the meantime, she didn't put it past Miss Kay to chase her all the way back to Chicago, on foot if necessary, so she increased her descent, taking two stairs at a time, and broke into the underground garage at a full sprint.

63.

Steel looked on gleefully as his mother came out of their room at a near run. She headed away from him and the stairs. He assumed the front desk clerk had called, announcing the arrival of a note that concerned her son. The rest was pure motherly instinct.

She turned and disappeared, heading down another hall toward the bank of elevators. Steel made his move. He pushed through the stairwell door, ran down the hall, and reached the room. His hand trembled as he inserted the key card, wondering what he'd do if Marshal Larson had waited inside. Thankfully, he found the room empty—or, more accurately, not quite empty.

He slipped FIDOE into a drawer, hoping his mother wouldn't look there. He then got what he'd come for and hurried back to the stairwell. He had no way of knowing what Kaileigh had gone through, but he *felt* an internal panic. They'd been crazy to try this.

Crazier still if they actually got away with it.

64.

Grym paced anxiously along a row of gray, rain-stained windows. On the other side of the wall a woman was tied to a chair, her hair disheveled, her cheeks stained with a mixture of tears and mascara. For the time being she was asleep—her chin touching her collarbone—a peaceful state she no doubt cherished.

Soon, Grym had to decide what to do with her; how to handle her. Where some captors might show mercy, Grym had other plans. Her existence offered him nothing but bad choices.

A faint voice at the back of his head told him he could let her go when this was over. She and her husband might report her kidnapping—although they'd be fools to, since his threat would be to come back and finish what he'd started—but even then they couldn't prevent the outcome without a great deal of proof that they did not have. The Power Poker lottery would be won by a person having no ties to any Chicago street gangs or terrorists—Joe Normal. Grym's brother was the only one who knew the man's identity. They compartmentalized such information whenever possible, in case of arrest. Grym awaited the phone call informing him that their person on the inside of the lottery commission had made the substitution. Their gang had leverage over such people, the result of complicated networking, underworld contacts, and the paying of favors. They'd been owed, and now they'd been paid. Or soon would be. That phone call would sound a starter's pistol in his head: once the switch was made, there was only one possible outcome: Joe Normal, with no traceable connections to their gang, would win more than forty million dollars. In six months' time that forty million dollars would be broken into eighty different parts and transferred several times before heading to the Middle East. But during that six months, the forty million would produce nearly one million dollars in interest—and this money was his gang's reward, theirs to keep. A million dollars could buy a lot of trouble, a lot of weapons—they'd be in business for years.

It might have occurred to him to try and keep the forty million for himself, but even Grym didn't know the identity of Joe Normal—didn't know how the code at the bottom of the Polaroid played into this. And besides, he would never cross his brother. It had been his idea, his plan—Grym was just implementing one part of it.

He turned and paced in the other direction. *But what to do with the preacher's wife?* Until that money was transferred, six months from now, she and her husband presented at least a faint threat to the success of the operation. Could he allow such a thing? If not, was he prepared to do what was necessary?

He continued pacing, his knees and the soles of his feet sore from it already. She didn't deserve to die: she'd done nothing to harm anyone.

But he wondered: *Is there any other choice?*

65.

Natalie Shufman was starving. By nothing more than blind luck she'd spotted Grym—whom she knew by face but not by name—at the science challenge. Having warned the mother to get the boy away from here, she'd then done the only thing that she could think of: she'd followed Grym. He'd tricked his way into a hotel room—the boy's or an accomplice's? From there he'd gone to Union Station.

At Union Station he'd located the briefcase—a discovery that had shocked her. From the train station he'd traveled by subway to this place. She'd spent the night in the same abandoned car as she was sitting in now. This morning he'd ventured out to a church—again, by subway—briefcase in hand.

He'd left the church without the case.

All this while she'd had nothing to eat.

Now she was hiding inside the abandoned car in what looked like a bombed-out neighborhood, where she doubted even the police went without backup. The street pavement was cracked and heaving; what had once been sidewalks were now weed patches. Most of the brick homes were abandoned, their windows busted out, their front doors covered with plywood, and the plywood spray painted with graffiti. A very old, and very thin three-legged dog gimped across the street, sniffing a dead squirrel in what looked to be its second week of decay. The only sounds were distant: traffic, a helicopter, and just beneath that, the unrelenting pulse of rap music.

Third building to the right was the one he had entered. It looked like an old mill or factory building: brick and glass and boarded up. He had been in there for two hours. It seemed a desperate place to hide. The heat had to be overpowering in there—windows all shuttered, many covered with graying plywood. She could imagine rats and spiders and the foul smells of stale air and rot.

She assumed there would be men coming to deal with the boy. She believed they would check in with this man first. She never questioned her determination, her resolve, to protect the boy. Had she been objective, she would have recognized the futility of it all. But it was a defense of innocence, more than anything: the boy didn't deserve whatever they had planned for him. She blamed herself for his involvement. Her own innocence had been stolen from her by people just like Grym; she wasn't going to allow the boy to be hurt.

That Grym knew about the science challenge, knew about the hotel, troubled her. His venturing *inside* the hotel room perplexed her. What did he have planned?

And what, if anything, could she do to stop him?

66.

"You're brilliant," Kaileigh said.

"I try," Steel said immodestly. Connected to the end of Steel's arm was a strap of purple nylon mesh—a leash—and attached to the leash was Cairo. "She has the nose of a bloodhound—that's the saluki in her—and the brain of a German shepherd. I got the idea for FIDOE from watching her sniff out rabbits in our backyard. The really good thing is, she doesn't run on batteries."

"But when your mom finds out . . ."

"Yeah, but I'm already in so much trouble it doesn't count."

"I think it will count," Kaileigh said with a smile.

"Yeah, you're probably right."

They arrived back at the L'Enfant Plaza Metro

station and stood in the exact location where FIDOE had run out of power. Steel scented Cairo on to the briefcase and then passed the briefcase to Kaileigh.

"We can throw it out now," Steel said.

"What?"

"We can't carry it when Cairo's trying to scent it. It'll confuse her. There's nothing in it we need."

"We can't just throw it out," Kaileigh said in a hush. "What if they need it later as . . . evidence?" She said this word in a complete whisper.

"Then set it down," Steel said. "Leave it here."

"Why?"

"Because this close to the entrance, they'll treat it as a threat: an unattended bag. They'll probably call the bomb squad or something, but you can be sure they'll take notice of it, and they'll lock it up somewhere."

She considered what he'd said. "You really *are* smart, you know?"

Cairo became excited.

"We can't keep it," he said.

Kaileigh walked over to a bench and set the case down. After all their efforts to find and hold on to it, it was difficult to just leave it behind. Both she and Steel glanced over their shoulders to look back as

Cairo led them onto and down the moving escalators, straining at the leash.

Once into the station, Cairo roamed in big, loopy circles, clearly having lost the scent, and for a moment Steel allowed himself to believe this had all been for nothing. But then her tail began wagging, her nose went lower to the concrete, and Cairo made for the turnstiles. The L'Enfant station was enormous, with several interconnecting lines. Steel glanced up: Cairo was pulling to enter the green line, which terminated at Branch Avenue.

"What tickets do I buy?" Kaileigh asked, panic rising in her voice. She stood in front of a sleek vending machine with blinking lights. The options proved intimidating. "How do we know where we want to get off? She's going to lose the scent once we're on the train."

"Buy two for the end of the line," he said. And she did.

Steel's plan took shape on the first stop: he and Kaileigh and Cairo got off the train. He walked Cairo from one end of the platform to the other, and he made sure to give the dog a good whiff of the exit. When Cairo failed to show any interest, it was pretty clear she'd lost the scent, because when Cairo had the scent you could barely hold her back.

As a precaution, they walked her over to the opposite platform and repeated the routine—up and down the platform. With the dog still showing no interest, they reboarded the train in the original direction, and got out at what was their second stop: Navy Yard.

The train departed, leaving them there. Steel patiently walked the dog from one end of the platform to the other.

Kaileigh said, "I understand the logic, Steel, but this could take forever." Another train arrived, and she said, "Let's get on. Please don't tell me we have to wait for another."

Steel said, "We can't. It's not scientific. We have to do the *exact* same procedure at each station, or the formula is flawed and the results will be inconsistent." Unable to tell if she'd heard him above the roar of passengers leaving the train, he turned toward her, worried she might board against his wishes. Above all, he didn't want to get separated.

Kaileigh hadn't been listening. She was staring up at a huge advertising poster. She had her head tilted back and her mouth was open, slack jawed. "Kaileigh!" Steel called out, but she didn't respond.

He glanced up at a sign: NEXT TRAIN: 2 MINS. She would insist they take this second train, so he hurried Cairo to the stairs that led to the bridge connecting the two platforms, determined to let Cairo sniff the other side. But halfway up the stairs, as Steel's attention remained on Kaileigh, the leash tightened, jerked, and pulled out of Steel's hand.

Cairo bounded up the stairs in a blur—at a full run. She tore across the bridge, following the exit signs, ignoring his repeated cries. "Cairo, Come! CAIRO, SIT!" But the dog headed straight for the escalators, her nose to the concrete.

She'd picked up the scent, he thought.

"KAILEIGH!"

Kaileigh remained staring up at the poster with a stupefied look on her face. From Steel's angle, he couldn't see which poster, but it hardly mattered. He had no choice but to follow Cairo—and to run as fast as he could. The dog entered the right-hand escalator, squeezing past people, *flying* up the stairs.

Steel hit the escalator running, the glow of daylight seen at the very top. But whereas Cairo didn't seem to even notice she was climbing eighty feet of stairs, Steel's legs quickly stiffened and became two lead weights. After only a short distance, his mighty effort had died and he was barely running at all.

That was when Kaileigh ran past him *taking two stairs at a time*. She even had enough wind to apologize to the people she'd slipped past and to scream once loudly: "Somebody stop that dog!"

Steel wasn't about to lose this particular race. He found a reserve he didn't know he had, his heavy legs back in action and—*one stair at a time*—he climbed the escalator. When he finally reached the top, his legs were throbbing. To his horror, Kaileigh had not waited for him; she was nowhere to be seen.

Cairo was gone.

Steel found himself alone, at the top of the Metro station, in an unfamiliar place, his plan gone astray, just like his dog.

67.

Larson descended the escalator at the Waterfront-SEU Metro station at a full run, Hampton right behind him. He'd gotten the call only minutes earlier: just after Larson's Be On Lookout, a young boy and girl and a dog—with no adults—had been spotted by a transit cop monitoring a closed-circuit television.

"It has to be them," Larson said over his shoulder.

"Look where you're going!" Hampton called back. One slip at this speed and Larson would go head over heels down fifty feet of steel stairs.

They were met at the bottom by two men in blue uniforms. The transit police introduced themselves, and one quickly said, "False alarm. When we called, we thought we had them crossing to the north platform. But they came back and got *back on* the southbound train."

"They what?" Hampton blurted out.

Larson tried to make sense of this. "You're sure there were three of them, and they were traveling together?"

"A young boy with a girl and dog. Just like the BOL you put out," the officer said.

"They got *off* the train," Hampton said. "Went over to the other platform, came *back* to the southbound platform, and got back on? What's that about?"

"That's what I'm saying. We called it in because we thought we had them. Mike, here—" he said, indicating his partner, "he headed up to the top of the tube to cut 'em off. But *wham*, there they were getting back on the dang train."

"What are they up to?" Larson muttered, trying to think this through. Then he said under his breath, "Why does this kid have to be so smart?"

Then he answered his own question. "The *dog*! They're trying to use the dog to—" He cut himself off. "The kid was concerned about the woman in the photo."

"But if they're trying to go after her . . . they're headed for trouble," Hampton said.

"So we'd better stop them." Larson studied the station, trying to make sense of the kids' movements. "They were being thorough: that's why they checked the other platform. They were using the dog to try to pick up a scent. That makes everything fit."

"That dog was not on a scent," the transit cop said. "I'm a hunter. I got bird dogs. I know when a hound is on a scent, and that dog may have been looking, but he wasn't getting anything."

"They're going station to station," Hampton said. "Somehow—don't ask me how—they know the guy took this line, and they're trying to pick up the scent again."

Larson tugged on one of the cops to join him. Together, they sprinted for the escalator. Larson instructed, "Call down the line, station to station, to be looking for them: a dog and two kids. They can't be too far ahead. We've *got* to find them." He reached the escalator, Hampton right behind him.

The transit cop watched the two men bounding up the long, long rise into the glowing circle of light above them.

"Did you hear me?" Larson hollered back down. "We've got to find those kids!"

68.

Steel had to find them: Cairo and Kaileigh had disappeared off the face of the earth. A few blocks from the Metro station the neighborhood turned dirty and run-down. The sidewalks were cracked, the streets in horrible shape—the kind of place where, in Chicago, his mother always locked the car doors and rolled up all the windows. He tried to look confident, but his anxiety overcame him as he walked past houses with small, unmowed lawns of brown grass sprinkled with litter. He passed a gleaming red convertible that held a couple of white guys smoking cigarettes in the front seat. They were covered in tattoos, and they looked at Steel like he was some kind of afternoon snack.

Where'd they go? he wondered. *How could a girl and*

a dog disappear so quickly? What if they were in trouble?

He was drawn by the sound of barking—a sound that kept moving. It wasn't Cairo's bark, but it could have been the result of Cairo passing by. First he heard it to his right, so he moved a block in that direction. He found some dogs behind a chain-link fence. They didn't bark as he passed, and he wondered, *Do they only bark at other dogs?* Then more barking came from up the street, and Steel ran to catch up.

He found these dogs as well, both German shepherds, one on a leash tied to a metal stake, the other on a front porch, too old and gray to go anywhere. Now, more barking in the distance. He looked out at old sofas on porches. A chair with the stuffing bubbling out of it. Houses in total disrepair, many of them boarded up. Did he dare to keep following the sounds of barking dogs deeper and deeper into this wasteland? He looked behind him; at least he wasn't lost: he had the ability to remember each and every turn he'd taken to get here.

But where was everybody? There wasn't a person on this street besides him, in either direction. There were a few old cars parked, but most of them weren't going anywhere—not if you needed tires, doors, or windshields. Of the cars that actually drove past him, most had dark, opaque windows and pulsed from the music that blared from within. They drove slow, like patrol cars, and reminded him of Cairo when she was out hunting. He felt like the prey. He felt a hundred eyes were trained on him, and yet he couldn't see a soul; he imagined people hiding behind the dark windows of the burned-out buildings and abandoned playgrounds.

What choice did he have but to follow the sound of barking? What other clues were there? He felt so angry at Kaileigh. Then his anger changed to concern, and from concern to fear. What if Kaileigh had caught up to Cairo? What if Cairo had led Kaileigh straight to the man from the train? What if she was now captured and Cairo along with her? What then?

The barking stopped. Silence sat atop the groan and grind of traffic and a distant city. All at once, Steel realized what a comfort the barking had been. Without it, this place seemed twice as dangerous, and he felt twice as desperate. His feet slowed; he wasn't so eager to go any deeper into this place. It felt like his science teacher's description of a black hole in space: matter went in but never came out. He didn't want any part of that.

Then he saw a distant brick building riddled with broken windows. It triggered something powerful in him, a vivid memory trapped in his mind. *What's it from?* He felt it was something important—critically important—if only he could understand . . . could place it. . . . He fought against his fear of this place, the terror that had taken over his mind. Pushed it away . . . back . . . back . . . trying to clear his thoughts. *"Don't get in your own way,"* his father had once told him, when coaching him for a science quest. *"Don't be your own worst enemy."*

He took a deep breath now, as he had then. He closed his eyes and pictured something peaceful: snow falling outside the window on a winter's day. Slowly the snow melted, and there was the image he was searching for: the preacher's wife tied to a chair; behind her and over her left shoulder, a row of windows—broken windows.

He saw each of the shapes distinctly, his memory locked on to the image: their ragged breaks and missing pieces. Five of them in a row, fairly high up the wall.

He opened his eyes. There, several blocks ahead, a brick building with all sorts of broken windows—the top rows of which were in groups of *five.*

He started running. He wanted to be closer, to reverse the image so clear in his mind and try to match windows to windows. He ran a block, crossed the street, and started down the next.

"Steel!" Kaileigh's voice called out.

Startled, he jumped fully off the ground, lost his balance, and crashed to the sidewalk. He quickly got up, scampered to his left, where Kaileigh, holding tightly to Cairo's collar, was hunkered down behind a leafless shrub. She was frantically waving at him.

"Where . . . How . . . ?" He couldn't catch his breath.

"I almost didn't catch her," Kaileigh explained in a forced whisper. "She was on the scent, and running *so fast*. But there were these dogs . . . and she slowed each time . . . and when I finally caught her leash, she nearly dragged me off my feet. I wasn't sure what to do—how to find you. And then you just showed up."

"It's the brick building," Steel said. "The guy from the train. Has to be." He told her about his memory of the windows in the photo.

"You can remember the *shapes* of the broken windows in the photo?" She sounded either impressed or doubtful; he couldn't tell which.

"I need to get closer," he said. "To check out every side of the building."

"I don't exactly love it here."

"No," he agreed. "What happened to you back in the station? You spaced out."

Her eyes went wide as if she'd forgotten about it until just now. "Oh, yeah! You wouldn't believe it! It was this lottery poster. Huge. Up on the wall of the station. You remember the billboard we saw from the balcony of your hotel room? It was sort of like that. You know the balls they use to spell out lottery: L-O-T-T-E-R-Y? Well, this poster had the same balls spelling it out the same way—only they were in this machine, this plastic cube, with a whole bunch of numbered balls. And I just *saw* it. You know? You know like when you're working on a math equation, or trying to think through a science assignment? You know that moment when you just *get it*? I know you do."

"Sure."

"It was like that!" She was excited, her face red, her eyes even wider. She spoke so quickly, Steel could barely stay with her. "All those Ping-Pong balls in that plastic box—and near the top of the box this tube—an opening that sucks out the winning numbers. It just took a minute for me, you know, to *see* it, to see the way it works: all the balls being blown around this box and then the tube sucking one of them up. It's my science challenge, Steel: the

Ping-Pong balls are just little balloons. Right? Just floating around in that box. Only the thing is, whichever balloon floats the highest is the one that gets sucked up—the one that gets counted. My project wasn't stolen by a competitor. It was stolen by these people. That guy from the train." She looked up at Steel with anger in her eyes. "They stole my project to rig the lottery."

For a moment, Steel couldn't breathe. It was if she'd sucked all the oxygen out of the air. He hadn't seen the poster, so he wasn't exactly sure what this box looked like. But he pieced it together from what she'd said: a box of Ping-Pong balls; an open tube near the top; the balls bouncing around.

"Could it be used for that?" he asked.

"What do you think I'm telling you? Of course it could! Remember, my project makes it possible to control which balloon floats the highest and for the longest. In the lottery, the highest Ping-Pong ball is the one that gets collected—gets counted as the winning number. You tweak my project a little, and instead of balloons, it's Ping-Pong balls, and instead of winning the science challenge, you win forty-five million dollars."

Steel processed this. "You're sure?" he asked.

"I promise you it's possible. Yes. Absolutely. The

train left from Chicago. That's where I live: just outside Chicago. That briefcase . . . for all we know it had something more than just that photo—like my notes, for instance. Like the whole thing laid out for them."

"How's it work?" Steel asked.

"You think I'm telling you? No way!"

"Kaileigh!"

She puckered her face in obstinacy and finally relented. "It's *so* ridiculously simple. All I did was take a computer chip—I salvaged my first one from one of my dad's old cell phones—and I use it to *warm* the gas—I used neon—inside the balloon. The chip is activated by any phone that has the walkie-talkie function. The chip picks up the transmission, turns itself on, and immediately warms. The gas warms with it. The balloon rises. Simple enough, but it works like magic."

"Forty-five million dollars' worth," Steel said.

"I'm thinking this gang, or whatever, read about my project in the newspaper and realized it could be used to rig the lottery. Stealing it from school was easy enough. They'd have to modify it some, and obviously they'd need someone to switch out their Ping-Pong balls with the ones usually used. So it's complicated, but they could do it."

"Okay, here's the plan," Steel said. "I've got to get a look at the windows of all four sides of that building."

"But what about Cairo? Isn't she enough?"

"She can help. If she scents that building, then we know we're there." Cairo wagged her tail as if she'd understood what he'd said. "But if I can identify the floor for them, then they'll know exactly where to look."

Cairo suddenly jerked to the left. It all happened too fast for Steel, whose mind was engaged with everything Kaileigh had been telling him.

"Are you crazy? He'll *kill* you." A woman's voice. Angry or frightened, Steel wasn't sure which.

Steel turned and looked up into the face of the woman from the train.

69.

Larson and Hampton were met at the Navy Yard Metro station by an overweight D.C. transit cop with tired eyes and two silver teeth. His name was Coleman, and he accompanied the two marshals to the bottom of the escalators.

"This is where I was when I first seen the dog. He come out of there like someone fired a starter's pistol—low to the ground and moving like a greyhound. Hit the escalator 'fore I could grab him."

"Just the dog?" Hampton said, clarifying.

"Then a girl, fast as greased lightning."

"And the boy?" Larson asked.

"Dead last," the man said. "Between him and the girl, I gotta say that he looked the most frightened—

the most upset. Like maybe the dog belonged to him."

"It does," said Hampton.

"They went up to street level," Larson said, verifying what he'd been told a few minutes earlier.

"Yes, sir. Up top, and they ain't come back down since."

Larson thanked the man. He and Hampton joined the escalator and climbed as quickly as they could, finally reaching street level.

"What now?" Hampton asked, looking around and seeing no sign of the kids. "They could be anywhere."

"If you'd kidnapped a woman," Larson said, "and you had her somewhere in this neighborhood, where would it be?"

"Where the fewest people lived," Hampton answered automatically. "Somewhere that gave me options for escape if people like us showed up."

"A remote location that's difficult to contain."

"You could put it that way," Hampton said.

Larson got his bearings and pointed north. "That direction, the neighborhoods steadily improve."

"But that way," Hampton said, indicating the opposite direction, "is Buzzard Point. A cousin of mine grew up there with his grandma. Not the most scenic part of our nation's capital."

"Navy Yard abuts the river. FBI used to have its field office down here in Buzzard Point. Tough neighborhood."

"What do you want to do?" Hampton asked.

"I want to find those kids before they find Grym," Larson said.

"Amen to that."

"We'll go on foot, but I think it's time to call in backup. Let's ask for a couple Metro Police patrols to drive these streets looking for two kids and a dog."

"I'm on it," Hampton said, flipping open his phone.

Larson spun once, slowly in full circle. There was little traffic and almost no pedestrians: few people, if any, to begin questioning. This was going to come down to footwork and luck.

Where are you? he wondered.

70.

Steel's first instinct was to run, but the woman had Cairo.

"Give her back," Steel said, on his feet and facing the woman.

"Not until you agree to go back to the hotel. I warned your mother . . ."

"And if we agree?" Kaileigh asked.

Steel shot her a look; he felt betrayed.

"This is dangerous for all of us," the woman said. "The farther away from here, the better."

"We know about the lottery," Steel said. "We know what you're up to."

"I don't have a clue what you're talking about," the woman said. She sounded sincere, and Steel didn't know what to think. "I'm in trouble, too, you know? I stuck my neck out to protect you. And now—"

"*Protect* me?" Steel said harshly. "I don't think so."

She looked scared. He wasn't sure if someone could fake that. Her eyes jumped around in her head like she was trying to look a hundred directions at once.

"I'm here because I believe there are people—bad people—after you," she told him. "That may be my fault, and there's nothing I can do about it now, except get you away from here. I tried to tell your mother to get you out of here. It's not my fault that she didn't listen. But I'm warning you . . ." She looked Steel and then Kaileigh right in the eye. "You do not want to get anywhere near this guy. This guy is the worst of the worst. Totally bad news."

"He has a lady. A hostage. A preacher's wife. We're going to find out where he is and call the police. It's that brick building, isn't it?" He pointed.

"Listen, Sherlock, this is *not* a game. It's not a video game," the woman said. "This guy is bad news, and he'll hurt you *and* your friend and your dog if he finds you. That's if you're lucky. You messed things up for him. And he is not the kind of person to forgive. He'll make an example of you." She whispered, "I think they mean to kill you, kid. Why do you think I stuck around?"

"Steel." Kaileigh had gone as white as Wonder Bread. "Let's just do as she says."

"How do we know it isn't a trap?" Steel said. He meant this for Kaileigh, but he never took his eyes off the woman, and more specifically, her hand holding Cairo's leash.

"How'd you get here?" the woman asked.

"The subway," Kaileigh answered.

"Shut up!" Steel told her.

"I'll walk you back to the subway," the woman said. "I'll give the dog back to you there." She apparently hadn't missed Steel's attention on his dog.

"I don't believe you," Steel said. "You lied to me in Chicago—said the briefcase wasn't yours. If you hadn't done that . . . If you'd just *taken* the stupid briefcase . . . But you lied. And that's the reason all this happened, so don't go blaming me. I'm not going anywhere with you."

"The briefcase wasn't mine," the woman said, angry with him now. "I was delivering it, is all. You stupid idiot. If you'd just left things alone . . ."

"He's going to kill the preacher's wife. If I'd left things alone, no one would know any of this."

"Listen, you know more than I do," the woman said, somewhat ashamed. "I was a mule."

"A mule?" Kaileigh said.

"A courier. I delivered the briefcase. That's all I was in for until you came along. But then . . . You want to save the world, kiddo, that's your business. You want your dog back?" She passed Steel the leash. "Okay. You've got the dog back. But you go into that brick building, and you're never coming out. Not alive, you aren't."

"Steel?" Kaileigh said. "I think we should listen to her."

"It's a trick," Steel said. He passed the leash to Kaileigh. "Don't let go."

"I'm outta here," the woman said. She turned and walked away. Away, not only from them, but from the brick high-rise as well.

"Wait!" shouted Steel, trying to stop her. "What floor are they are on?"

"No clue," she said without looking back. "And I do *not* care." Then she stopped and turned. "You're making a big mistake. I'm getting out of here. That's where I'm starting: staying alive. I'm not going to stay here debating with you. But trust me, you're crazy if you go into that building. And *you*," she said to Kaileigh, "have the right idea. Get the heck out of here. The guy in there is nothing but trouble."

"I need to circle the building," Steel said, pleading with Kaileigh. "Not get inside, only circle around it. We'll leave here after that."

"No," the woman said. "That's a stupid idea. What if he sees you? No way."

"Steel, I think she's right," Kaileigh said.

"If I leave, there's no way that marshal is going to let me come back here. And they won't know what floor she's on. What room she's in. That means there'll be no way to sneak up on that guy. And if he hears them going room to room, or sees them or something, who knows what he'll do to the woman in the chair?" He spoke to the stranger. "It's like you said: he's a bad person. He could do anything to her. Are we supposed to just let that happen?" He paused. "I can't do that."

He looked at Kaileigh. "If you have to leave, I totally get it. No problem. Do what you've got to do. But I've got to take a lap around that building whether that's risky or not. Take Cairo to the station. I'll meet you there, if you wait for me."

"No way."

"Way."

"If you're staying, I'm staying," Kaileigh said.

She glanced over at the woman with a worried expression.

"The more of us, the worse it is," Steel said. "I get that much. He knows about Cairo. Maybe not about you. But if he sees a couple of kids and a dog, he's going to know it's us. One kid walking alone is a lot less likely to draw attention." Steel looked to the woman for support.

"You're crazy," the woman said.

"Maybe. Yeah, you're probably right," Steel said. "But you and that briefcase started this, not me." Excited and scared at the same time, he had to get moving. Standing in one place was not happening. "Give me twenty minutes," he told Kaileigh. "If I'm not at the station in twenty minutes, get back and find my mother, and tell Larson everything."

Cairo pulled at the leash, trying to follow the scent that still drew her. Kaileigh looked as if she might cry. She tugged at the dog, and finally Cairo followed her off in the direction of the station.

71.

Steel was no hero. He wasn't doing this to prove something. He just couldn't leave without gathering all the information available. It was like the lady tied in the chair was a science project he had to complete.

The sidewalk had decayed into fragments of concrete and trapezoids of bare dirt—a jigsaw puzzle with pieces missing. The curb looked as if some kind of bacteria had eaten it away. Still a block and a half from the brick high-rise, Steel kept his left shoulder nearly touching the decayed storefronts—a former Laundromat, its windows missing; what had once been a corner store now looked like a bombed-out bunker. The closer he drew to the building, the more it dominated the sky, its rows of broken windows like unrelenting eyes looking down on him.

He stopped, hidden partly behind a bashed and dented refrigerator that stood improbably on the corner like a phone booth. *Click, click*: he captured the rows of windows on the building's north side and tried to match them with what he'd seen in the Polaroid of the preacher's wife. He remembered to flip the image in his mind's eye, knowing he was searching for the reverse image. Nothing he saw fit the pattern.

He mentally grabbed them in groups of four—the number of windows behind the hostage in the photo. Grabbed them; flipped them; compared them. But the process was painstakingly slow, for he knew it could be any combination of any four windowpanes in a single line. His mind tired with the effort—it was worse than the memorization games he'd played to impress his friends and teachers. His brain was like an overloaded computer—it heated up. He got a headache.

He looked ahead to the end of the road and the dark brown waters of the river, where a lonely barge moved slowly behind the effort of a tugboat. This was the only sign of human life. His anxiety burned a hole in his stomach. He thought he might puke. He looked the other way. No Kaileigh. No woman.

No Cairo. Gone. Just an empty street lined with empty houses.

What was he doing here? What had he been thinking?

He came to the end of this block and crossed again, reaching a bent and twisted railing that rode a seawall at the end of an empty parking lot, the river's water churning only a few feet away. He turned to look back at the south-facing wall of the abandoned brick structure and its row after row of vandalized windows.

His eye picked it out like a string of letters in a word scramble. The kind where the word is spelled backward and the grouping of letters is tucked into the second line from the bottom. But his eye saw it without any kind of prompting for analysis: four windows that when flipped left to right created the *exact* geometrical pattern he'd committed to memory the first time he'd seen that Polaroid.

And there, in the second window over: a pair of eyes. *His* eyes. Only the eyes. No face. No hair. No body to go with them.

Steel felt his lungs freeze. He couldn't have been more exposed: standing all alone against a railing in a crippled parking lot. It had been the only place from which to get a decent look at the east wall, but now that he saw where he was, he realized he couldn't have been more stupid. It might have been okay had he just kept his head down and walked along—a dejected kid walking along the seawall. But he'd been caught facing the building—*studying the building*—drawn to it by his brain's uncanny ability to decipher geometric shapes.

He heard rapid footsteps to his left—a person running. He looked but saw no one.

When he looked again for the eyes in the window, they were gone. Panic stung him. The man from the train was coming after him. He felt certain of this. He *knew* it with absolute conviction.

He had to pick a way out from the dead end he'd put himself into: the subway station was a long way off. Which side of the building would the man use to try to intersect Steel's escape route? Left or right? West or east? He had to outguess him.

Wait a second! he thought. If it was the man from the train chasing him, then wouldn't the hostage have been left alone? Wasn't this the perfect time to go inside and find her?

Steel caught movement out of the corner of his eye: a man running toward him from his left.

It was much too soon to be the man from up in

the window. *Then who?* Steel wasn't going to stick around and make introductions.

He sprinted for the nearest door of the abandoned building.

72.

Steel tried the door: locked. He kicked at it, but it held firm. He fought the urge to look back as he fled to his right.

He rounded the corner, very much aware that the man was still behind him. It wasn't a door he spotted, but a sheet of gray plywood, one corner warped and no longer screwed into the window frame. Steel yanked on the plywood and peeled it open just wide enough to slip through.

He dropped down off a ledge and into a puddle of water. Light seeped in around the perimeter of each piece of plywood, leaving a dozen glowing frames on the wall. It was enough light to make out the immediate area, a lobby or large office space, with square pillars set at regular intervals. The squishy thing beneath his shoes was a soggy carpet. Light fixtures hung bent off the wall like beckoning fingers.

The windows he'd spotted were five stories up. He hurried to the end of the room and pushed through a pair of swinging doors, entering into a dark corridor. Behind him he heard his pursuer kicking a door. It raised the hair on the nape of his neck. Then he heard the screech of plywood—the man was close. . . .

Steel tried one door after another—all locked—before finally spotting a rusted panel to the right of a steel door indicating a stairway.

He leaned a shoulder into the stairway door and it came open, revealing a dimly lit stairwell. He pushed the door shut behind him and took off up the stairs.

He passed cigarette butts, matchbooks, and fast-food litter. The light was dim, coming from somewhere high above. The air stank.

Up . . . up . . . up he went, as fast as he could run. He passed an exit door at each level bearing a huge block-printed number:

2

3

And then, from behind him, came the rapid slap, slap, slap of heavy feet.

Steel took two stairs at a time. If he could just make it to the next level, maybe . . . His legs burned. His pursuer was moving fast now, quickly closing the distance between them.

Steel knew what to do. He would surprise the man by turning and kicking out at just the right moment.

He slowed enough to allow his pursuer to gain on him.

Just as he reached the fourth-floor landing, he turned, grabbed the rail, and kicked out. He caught the man squarely in the chest with the sole of his shoe. His knee locked. The man didn't simply lose his balance, he *flew* off the stair. Launched into midair.

The man was carrying a small but powerful flashlight. Its beam wobbled, a circle of bluish white light danced on the dripping undersides of the stairwell above them. Then, as the man fell, Steel got a good look at the man.

It was his father.

73.

Kaileigh regretted having left Steel behind. He was the only friend she'd had for days now. Walking along with the woman—*a complete stranger*—she worried she'd done the wrong thing. She couldn't sort out what was wrong and what was right. If Cairo hadn't been there, she'd have been even more scared, but just the presence of the dog calmed her some.

"That's about the twentieth time you've looked back," the woman said.

"I'm worried about him."

"He made his choice," the woman said. "He'll have to live with it. Or not."

"Don't say that."

"I warned him."

"I should have stayed."

"Two wrongs . . ." the woman offered. "He's the one making the bad decision, not you."

But Kaileigh wondered. She knew very little about this woman, and what she did know wasn't the most reassuring: a gang member, a criminal. What had she done, agreeing to go off with her? What if the woman was trying to kidnap her?

"I can find the station from here by myself," she said.

"In this neighborhood? I don't think so."

She wanted to turn around and find Steel; she wanted to jerk on Cairo's leash and take off. But how far would she get? The woman had longer legs and looked to be fit and athletic. She wouldn't make it far.

She looked around, searching for some way out of this.

At that exact moment, two men jumped out at them. They had guns.

"U.S. Marshal," the taller man announced in a deep, thundering voice.

"Hands on the back of your head!" said the other.

74.

"Dad?" Steel's voice echoed in the bottomless chamber of the stairwell.

His father's face twisted into a knot of pain, where he lay head down on the stairs. His grimace tightened further as his hand jabbed beneath his back. Steel thought he'd torn a muscle or injured himself. But instead, his dad's hand quickly came out from beneath him, *holding a gun*.

"Steel! DUCK!" his father roared.

It took Steel several milliseconds to process the command, but perhaps because it came in his father's voice, he obeyed without a second thought. He allowed his knees to go weak, and, losing his balance, he tumbled forward.

His father fired two rounds from the gun:

right where Steel had been standing.

As Steel rolled, he heard the door thump shut, realizing too late that someone had been standing *right behind him* on the landing. His father had just shot at the man, but the door was shut now, and Steel hadn't heard the man scream with pain.

His father had a gun. His father . . . a gun . . . He had *fired* the gun. His father, the salesman turned FBI agent, acting like Alex Rider.

Kyle Trapp limped up the stairs and helped Steel to a sitting position. What his mother had told him about his father hadn't fully registered until this moment. It was as if he had to experience it for himself.

"I thought it was you! I nearly called out, but I only saw your back. . . ." his father said, panting. Beads of sweat ran down his face. "But it *is* you! And I need you to stay here."

"No!" Steel said, grabbing for his father's arm. "The woman in the chair . . . the preacher's wife . . . she's in this building."

"Okay . . . I'm on it!" his father said.

"You really are an FBI agent?" Steel said.

His father couldn't hide his surprise. "Your mother told you," he said, making it a statement, not a question. "Listen, we'll get to that."

His father continued up the stairs.

"I promise!" he called back.

"I am *not* staying here," Steel called out, stopping him. "Besides, I know which room she's in."

His father turned, out of breath. "This is what I do, Steel. It's dangerous. You've got to—"

"Come with you," Steel said, interrupting, "because I'm sure not staying here alone."

"Which room?"

"I'll show you."

Uncertainty hung between them: his father's sense of urgency, Steel's determination not to be left behind by his father yet again.

His father yielded. "Okay, but you stay *behind* me. And if I say drop, you drop."

"Yes, sir." Steel hurried up the stairs. "Not there," he said, seeing his father's hand on the door handle. "Fifth floor, facing east: the river." He could feel his father's eagerness to pursue the man he'd shot at—presumably the man from the train. And there was something else: a flicker of a father's doubt, not believing Steel. But this was quickly overcome by the fact that it was Steel, not just any boy. His father nodded.

"Fifth floor," he said, repeating what Steel had said. "Facing east."

"If he was trying to get up there, we just cut him

off. He'll have to go to the other side of the building. We've got the advantage."

"Run," his father said, taking off up the stairs at an amazing speed. Since when could his father move like that? It was as if his whole world had flipped upside down: his father an FBI agent, with a *gun*, chasing some gang lord in a bombed-out building in Washington, D.C.

"Is this really happening?" Steel blurted out, wondering if maybe everything from the train ride on had been some mixture of dream and nightmare, and that he was still asleep, still stuck in dreamland.

"Shh!" his father said.

Only then did he realize how silently his father climbed the stairs. He was floating instead of clomping. They'd lied to him! His mother and father had orchestrated a lie that must have gone back years. *A salesman*. The thing about it was, Steel had never pictured his father as a salesman. It had never made any sense. He knew too much about so many things; he had a childlike sense of adventure; he was an expert camper and outdoorsman. Weren't salesmen supposed to be boring and stuck in a rut? His father was anything but.

"Spy Kids!" he blurted out. "This is just like *Spy Kids*!" He thought about that for a second. *Only it's real.*

His father had one hand on the door to level five. The other—the hand with the gun—came to his lips and indicated silence.

He pulled open the door, peered out into the hall, and signaled Steel forward. Steel heard it before his father did: footsteps to their left. Steel signaled by pointing furiously. His father picked up on it, nodded, and used hand signals to indicate they would split up: Steel to the right, his dad to the left.

Steel figured the footsteps were the man from the train—hurrying to beat them to the preacher's wife. He got his bearings, recalling with absolute clarity the layout of the building from the outside. The tall panel of brick that rose in the middle of the east-facing wall would be the staircase they'd just left. The windows that matched the photograph were to the right. The same direction his father was sending him. Steel took off down the hall. His father ran off in the opposite direction.

He reached a door and pushed it open: *empty*. No, not empty, he realized. Fresh cigarette butts on the floor; fresh fast-food litter and empty soda cans on the table. Another door to his right. He hurried over to it and—*yes!*—it was secured with a padlock. He shouldn't have been so excited to find it locked, but the lock was *new*, and that could mean only one thing.

He kicked at the door, but the lock and hasp didn't budge. Again, but with the same results. He thought back to science class: leverage. He needed something long and strong to pry the lock's hasp off the door. There was an old wobbly chair by the table—but it was too big and bulky. There wasn't much else to the room—some junk piled in the corner.

Bam! A gunshot from down the hall. Then loud noises like a chase. Steel froze at the sound of the shot, briefly unable to breathe, much less move. But then that gunshot served as a starter's pistol for Steel. He raced to the far end of the room, kicked up at a broken window, and ripped a metal divider from the frame. He couldn't believe the thing was in his hand—but there it was. He shoved it between the hasp and the door and pulled against it. The hasp bent like a coat hanger. He shoved the metal prod deeper between the hasp and the door and pulled again. The screws began to show. Again. The screws grew in length, literally ripping from the wood door. At once, a piece of the doorjamb broke off, the wood frame splintering. The lock—still locked—and the hasp tore free, and Steel threw open the door.

The woman from the photograph, the preacher's

wife, was bound to the chair exactly as he'd seen her. The same geometrical pattern of broken windows were behind her on the wall. The room smelled of sewage—a disgusting bucket of filth next to a roll of toilet paper in the corner. Her eyes were open, but she didn't seem to see. Then she blinked, and tears ran from her eyes.

Steel said, "Don't worry, it's only me, Steel. My dad . . . he's back there. He's got a gun." He immediately went to work on the duct tape on her forearms, not understanding why he was saying what he was saying, but his mouth just gushing all this stuff. "I found the briefcase. I have this dog, Cairo. We came on the subway. My friend Kaileigh and me." He got her left arm free and started on her right, as she worked on the tape that covered her mouth.

"My prayers . . . my prayers . . ." she muttered. She was crying something fierce, coughing and gagging in a wet, disgusting display, while Steel was on his knees clawing at the duct tape that bound her ankles.

The noise from the hall grew closer: someone running.

Steel worked furiously. The last piece of tape came free.

When he pulled her out of the chair, the woman

fell, and Steel caught her. He found himself hugging this older woman—his face in her chest, her skin all blubbery and soft. He nearly puked. She found her legs and came to standing, using Steel to support her.

The men came through the door in the other room: his father and the guy from the train. A tangle of limbs. Fists flailing. They rolled on the floor. Steel saw his father take a bad blow to the face. Then another. Steel didn't mean to do it—it was nothing he thought about—but all at once he let go of the preacher's wife. She sank to the floor like a balloon sculpture losing air. He crossed into the room and headed straight for the wobbly-looking chair, picked it up and, as the man from the train wrestled into a position where he sat on top of Steel's father, delivering one fist after another into his father's swollen face, Steel hoisted the chair high over his head and lowered it onto the man's back with all his strength. The man sagged and fell, then raised to his elbows and dragged himself toward the windows. He rocked his head once in Steel's direction, his eyes filled first with rage and then disbelief as he seemed to gain focus.

"You?" he said.

Steel's father struggled to his feet. So did the man

from the train, who looked once at Steel and the chair, then at Steel's father. And then, totally unexpectedly, he turned and dove out the window—glass shattering in an enormous splash.

Steel and his dad ran to the window. The man was facedown in what had once been grass, far below. For a second it looked as if his right leg had disappeared, but then Steel realized it was broken at the knee and bent back beneath the man at an impossible angle. He rose to his elbows and actually started dragging himself toward the river.

"Help her!" his father yelled as he ran, limping, from the room. Steel heard the clatter of metal: his father had retrieved his gun. And then the bang of the stairway door and the thundering thumping of his father descending the stairs.

Steel got his shoulder under the woman's arm and helped her to standing. "You're going to be okay," he said. "We're going to get you out of here."

75.

Steel, his dad, Larson, and Kaileigh all passed through the office building's security. Larson and Mr. Trapp were required to remove their guns and run their sport coats through the X-ray machine. The building's lobby was open and rose several stories overhead so that everything echoed inside, from footsteps to voices.

Steel's dad had explained that because of his position with the bureau he couldn't allow his face to be seen by the press, or on TV, and that because of this, neither Steel nor he would receive any credit for what they'd done. There was, in fact, no mention of the rescue in the news. Grym, who was refusing to speak to the authorities or even his own attorneys, was being held somewhere, though Steel's dad wouldn't say where. It was all secrets within secrets, as far as Steel was concerned. He'd been disqualified from the science challenge. His mother was packing up at the hotel. It promised to be a long train ride home.

"So, I don't get it," Steel said. "How do you two know each other?" There'd been something between Larson and his father from the moment they'd connected—which had been only minutes behind Steel's rescue of the preacher's wife. But only now did Steel realize it meant something.

Larson looked over at Kyle Trapp, leaving the explanation to him.

To the surprise of both Kaileigh and Steel, Marshal Larson wanted to explore Kaileigh's theory about how the lottery might be rigged. And that was what had brought them all to this office building on a Sunday evening, only hours after the rescue, and less than three hours before the end-of-the-week drawing for the forty-five-million-dollar grand prize.

As they rode the elevator, Kyle Trapp explained.

"I was on your train, Steel. From Chicago to here."

Stunned, Steel couldn't get out a word.

"Marshal Larson discovered me," his father

continued. "I couldn't reveal my assignment because technically I didn't exist. A small plane I was flying to Chicago . . . But that's another story for another time. I was on the train to keep an eye on you and your mother because we—the FBI—had learned that Aaron Grym was believed to be taking that train. Marshal Larson was working with the same intelligence."

"But Mom—" Steel said, as if he hadn't heard any of this. He wanted to protect his mother, and his father played along.

"I couldn't tell her. Or you. Wanted to, but couldn't. I didn't know about you and the briefcase, or I'd have made you get off the train. Marshal Larson and I . . . if we'd both been able to tell each other our half of the story . . . But it didn't work out that way. And that led me to the challenge. We got word that Grym had lost the briefcase. The rest you know."

Steel wasn't sure what to say. Part of him felt angry, the other part relief. It had worked out okay. Grym had been caught and was in jail. So was Natalie Shufman, though his father had told him she was likely to be set free for trying to help Steel.

"You and Kaileigh—" his father said, his eyes

filled with appreciation and thanks. He was cut off by the elevator doors opening.

They were met on the eleventh floor by an officious-looking bald man with pale skin and bad breath. He led them into a bland office that had something to do with the District of Columbia's local government, and found chairs for everyone but Larson, who remained standing.

Mr. Cunningham was his name. He listened intently to Larson's explanation for the meeting, and then somewhat distractedly to Kaileigh's nervously energetic description of her science project.

"And your theory would be all well and good, young lady," Mr. Cunningham said, "except that the Ping-Pong balls we use are all carefully weighed and tested every Friday before closing. We then lock them in a vault until the drawing."

"But they would test okay," she said. "That's the thing . . . That's what they would have had to work out. They aren't going to substitute four or five balls, they're going to swap out every single one of them. And when you weigh them, they're all going to weigh the same, so they're going to pass your test."

"I can't unlock that vault," Mr. Cunningham said, "even for the Marshals Service, or the FBI. It would take a court order to open that vault, and I should inform you that the vault itself is on a time lock. From four p.m. Friday, when we last test the balls, to six forty-five p.m. Sunday—fifteen minutes before the weekly drawing—that safe can't be opened even if we wanted to. And that's for *exactly* this reason." He ran a hand across his bald head and looked around his desktop as if expecting a cup of coffee to appear. Or maybe something stronger. "The time lock eliminates any opportunity for sabotage over the weekend. Believe me, we know how important a fair and just lottery is to the credibility of the system. We do everything in our power to see it is kept that way."

Steel felt a need to speak up. "But what if someone, *on Friday*, switched out the entire group of balls before they were tested? How would you ever know?"

This seemed to perplex Mr. Cunningham. He hummed and coughed and said, "I find that *highly* unlikely."

"But not impossible," Steel's dad said.

Larson said, "We believe this jackpot may end up in the hands of terrorists, Mr. Cunningham. We need that safe opened now. This is a matter of national security."

"First, I couldn't open the safe now, even if I wanted to. As I just told you, it's on a time lock. Second, you will need a court order, perhaps several court orders to get any closer than fifty feet from those Ping-Pong balls. They are *never* handled, touched, or dealt with in any way prior to the drawing. Even the oil from your finger could give weight to one more than another. We're quite aware of all the pitfalls and opportunities for sabotage. This is a scientific process, sir, and we approach it scientifically. I'm sorry. But in one hour—at six forty-five," he said, checking the wall clock, "those Ping-Pong balls are going directly from the safe to the hopper—and that's all there is to it."

They waited as a group in the hallway while Larson tried desperately to raise the necessary judges to advance a court order and seize the lottery balls for examination. His description of a thirteen-year-old girl's science project made one judge laugh and hang up, believing it to be a prank. The hands of the clock continued their march around the numbers, and it became clear to all that they were doomed to failure.

At 6:43, Steel's photographic memory came to their aid. "Security!" he said, breaking nearly five minutes of silence when Larson's last attempt at a warrant had failed. He won everyone's attention.

"There are two ways to go with this," he said. "First, if Mr. Cunningham won't let us touch the Ping-Pong balls, what if we were to X-ray the case? We could see through the balls—to see if they're chipped out the way Kaileigh says they'd have to be—*without* ever touching them. Without ever opening the box."

"I like that!" Larson said.

"Good thinking," his father said.

"He'll never let us do it," Kaileigh said. "There's a procedure they follow to keep things honest. This won't fit in that procedure. Besides, there are inks that can be made to carry atomic weight by exposing them to radiation. Did you know that? That would give weight to the Ping-Pong balls, if something like that was being used. He's never going to allow it."

"I agree," said Steel, surprising them all. "Which is what brings me to my second option." He waited until he had the three of them looking at him and listening. He lowered his voice. "Kaileigh's project is very simple in execution. A phone chip receives a call. The chip warms, the interior gas expands, and the balloon rises. But a phone signal is required to wake up the chip—to warm the chip."

"Cell phones!" Kaileigh said.

"Exactly," Steel said. "Someone has to instigate five calls—one for each ball they want to rise—or the winning number won't match."

"And isn't there a delay in some of the TV broadcasts?" Kaileigh said. "It can't be someone watching from home."

"Someone in the room," Larson said.

"The drawing is done before a live audience," Steel's dad said. "Thirty or forty people. That's supposed to make it look more honest."

Steel said, "Everyone with a cell phone will have to pass it through security. They'll be X-rayed downstairs."

"Doors open at six forty-five," Steel's dad said.

"It's televised live. That means cameras. We can watch the people in the audience . . ." But Larson was already out of his chair.

It was as if he and Steel's dad could communicate without speaking.

Mr. Trapp said, "I'll take the security X-ray. I'll need Steel—*for his memory*. We will identify every person in the audience who has a cell phone. You take Kaileigh. Get a camera on the audience. Ten minutes!" he said. "We've got *ten minutes*!"

76.

Steel and his dad stood on the far side of the security checkpoint's X-ray monitor as the lottery audience was admitted into the building. Steel took in every face of every person who arrived with a cell phone. To his discouragement, that was twenty-six of the thirty people who showed up. He committed each face to memory, but knew he would be of little help when the time came.

He whispered to his father, "Why don't we just convince Mr. Cunningham to take everyone's cell phones before the drawing?"

"If we could convince Mr. Cunningham of anything, we would convince him of that. The problem is, Steel, some people just aren't believers."

"The thing of it is," Steel said, "the drawing

happens fast, doesn't it? They don't wait around. Is it even possible for someone to dial a phone that quickly? Punch in all those numbers in time? I doubt it."

"The numbers would have to be preprogrammed into the phone. That's not complicated. You can program most phones to speed dial from the keypad. One touch."

"And if that's the case," Steel said, "the person wouldn't even need to take his phone out of his pocket. Which means we aren't going to see that person even with our camera pointed at the audience."

"You're saying we can't do this?" his father asked.

"We're going about it the wrong way," Steel said. He watched as the last of the audience members moved toward the elevators. He checked his father's watch: 6:52. At 7:00 the drawing would start. Eight minutes.

"We know several things," Steel said to his father. "The chips in those Ping-Pong balls—if there are chips in there—were either purchased or stolen, probably in Chicago when they were figuring out how to adapt Kaileigh's science project to rigging the lottery. But long-distance calls, even on cell phones, take a few seconds to get through. It's unpredictable. What if the connection is weak or the system is busy? Besides that, the chips are inside the Ping-Pong balls, and have basically no antennas. How can these people be absolutely sure the calls will arrive quickly, and on time?"

"I don't have an answer to that," his father said.

"I'm just thinking aloud, Dad," Steel said. "The point is, it's too variable. The balls are picked quickly, one right after another. You can't depend on cell phones to dial fast enough, or even to get through."

"So?"

"So the way I'd do it is I'd have a radio transmitter—something *in the room* that would allow me to send out specific frequencies, one right after another. A high-frequency generator . . ." Steel felt a jolt of electricity pass through him. "They've modified her technology!" he said excitedly. "It's not cell phone frequencies. They can't control that in the room. It's Bluetooth."

"What?" His father sounded confused.

"Bluetooth, Dad. Wireless communication. Basically every cell phone has it these days. But it's only the PDAs that are going to let you mess with what frequencies you want."

"How many PDAs came through security, Steel?"

Steel squinted his eyes shut. "Two. A BlackBerry and a Motorola Q. The Q is Windows Mobile. It could be modified to do this—I know it could. The BlackBerry's more limited."

"Do you have a face to go with the Q? Did you get a face?" his father asked anxiously.

Steel squinted again. He saw the face: a normal-looking man with dark hair and glasses. "I've got it," he said.

77.

Mr. Trapp called up to Larson while he and Steel rode the elevator.

His watch read 6:56 p.m.

"Is that accurate?" Steel asked.

"A minute slow, a minute fast. I have no idea."

They were met in the hall by Larson and Kaileigh, and together the four entered the studio, where across the way they could see Mr. Cunningham flanked by two uniformed police officers. He held a box in his hand.

"Two minutes!" a stage manager shouted out. "Audience: quiet, please!"

The stage manager waved Cunningham onto the stage. He opened the box and poured the Ping-Pong balls into the plastic container. He shut the container's lid, someone threw a switch, and the balls started jumping around in the forced air inside the box.

"Steel?" his father asked.

"I don't see him," Steel answered. Face by face he'd gone through the small crowd. They sat in folding chairs on risers that looked down on the small stage where a man and a woman, both dressed in formal wear, awaited their cues to start the drawing. "He's not here."

"He has to be here," Larson mumbled. "What's the number again?" he asked Kaileigh. "The winning number?"

She recited it for him. He scribbled it down and crossed the stage to Cunningham. "This is the number that's going to win," Larson told him. "And when it does, I would hope you'd have a question or two about how we knew that *in advance*."

Cunningham looked dazed.

"ONE MINUTE!" a voice shouted.

"Come on, Steel," his father said, clearly frustrated.

"He's not in the audience," Steel said, still scanning the faces.

"Maybe you just don't remember right," said his father.

It was the first—and only—time his father had challenged his memory skills.

"He's not in the crowd, Dad," Steel said bluntly.

"Closed circuit," Kaileigh said. She pointed at the monitor they were watching. "Closed-circuit TV. It's not broadcast; it's real time. There's no delay. He doesn't have to be in the audience. He just has to have a view of one of these monitors."

"But they're everywhere," Mr. Trapp said.

It was true—there were a half dozen TV monitors spread around the studio, and twice that number of places someone could hide—behind a curtain, a prop—and not be seen.

"Spread out," his father said.

"TEN SECONDS!" The same loud voice.

The four of them fanned out, walking behind the cameras, but turning to try to take in all the locations of the TV monitors. Cunningham waved at them to stay quiet for the sake of the broadcast.

"FIVE, FOUR, THREE . . ."

A booming voice. "Good evening! And welcome to the Sunday night lottery!"

Steel worked past the cameras, to the right of the audience. He caught a glow of light coming from behind a stage curtain directly across from him. The set was basically dark except for that blue glow at waist height in the middle of a curtain. A PDA? he wondered.

"And the first number is . . ."

Steel mouthed the number as the announcer said it:

"Seven!"

The audience applauded. Now Steel had no doubt. It was rigged: Kaileigh had been right.

"Tonight's second number is . . . *two*."

Steel ducked under the camera's sight line, crossing the set. To his right, Cunningham stared dumbfoundedly down at the piece of paper Larson had handed him. The man looked up, confused, and nearing a state of panic.

There! He caught another glimpse of dull blue light. The curtain rippled: there was a man back there. Steel tackled the hanging curtain the way he'd been taught in football: low and hard, driving his shoulder forward, head down.

"TONIGHT'S THIRD NUMBER . . ."

He hit something hard and muscular. And strong. He went down, as did the man. The curtain tore and fell down onto them. He heard the *clackety-clack* of something scooting across the floor.

His dad and Larson were alongside him in seconds, untangling the curtain and pinning the man under it. Kaileigh scurried across and picked up the PDA—a Motorola Q cell phone. She fumbled with it and pulled out its battery. The device went dark.

"Tonight's fifth number . . ." Steel had missed the calling out of the fourth. ". . . is *eight*."

Steel, being helped to his feet by his dad, met eyes with Kaileigh. This fifth number was incorrect. *Four* was the number in the code. They'd done it—the winning number had not been picked.

The two cops raced over and helped out. The man was handcuffed and brought to his feet. Behind a roar of audience applause, the quick drawing went off the air.

Cunningham marched over to Larson and said, "You nearly wrecked the drawing, Marshal. Your superiors will be hearing from the proper authorities. And as for this so-called winning number: you weren't even right!" He tore up the piece of paper, and confetti fell to the ground.

Kaileigh and Steel could no longer contain themselves. They broke out laughing.

78.

MONDAY, JUNE 2

They met the next day in the waiting area of Union Station, which seemed only fitting to Steel since he'd met Kaileigh on the train in the first place. She was in the care of Miss Kay, who looked more pleasant up close, though not without a certain old-school posture and pursing of the lips. They were booked on the same train back to Chicago. Once again Steel's dad was not going to make the trip. He had to stay behind to write reports and give statements about all that had happened.

The man caught at the lottery drawing was found with the winning ticket in his wallet—the ticket that Larson and Hampton had traced to its sale at a convenience store. A ticket that had nearly been worth forty-five million dollars. Every Ping-Pong ball in the lottery was found to have a phone chip inside, and investigations were underway to uncover who had switched out the rigged Ping-Pong balls for the originals. No connection could be made between the man arrested and Aaron Grym, also under arrest. The man at the lottery was charged with attempted robbery and conspiracy to defraud the federal government, but he was unlikely to spend more than a few years in prison.

Grym had been taken to a hospital and later transferred to a city jail, awaiting a hearing and further transfer to a federal facility. There was no mention of him, or a briefcase, or a young woman in the news. It was as if none of what Steel had gone through had ever happened. There was one brief article on someone trying to rig the lottery, but that was all.

The science challenge was won by a dimple-faced, goofy-looking boy who, in his picture on the front page of the business section, wore a Hawaiian shirt. Steel remembered the nervous boy, and he smiled at his victory. Steel hoped to compete in next year's challenge, though his own future was currently in question.

Steel said good-bye to Cairo, crated and ready for transport to the baggage car. They'd arranged adjacent sleeper cars so that Kaileigh and Steel could spend time together.

The two days on the train passed uneventfully. More than once, Steel had been cautioned to pay no attention to any briefcases or misplaced luggage, but he needed no encouragement. He and Kaileigh spent time with her computer, or playing cards, or reading. He didn't want to admit it, but he had no problem with her being a girl, and he felt closer to her than friends he'd had most of his life.

So when it came time in Chicago to say good-bye, the words came with difficulty.

"I don't know exactly how to say this," Steel said.

"That's because you're a science nerd," Kaileigh interjected.

"Yeah . . . but the thing is . . . in a weird way, I had a really good time."

"A very weird way."

"Obviously."

"Me too," she said. "And I'm sure we'll see each other again. You're going to the regionals in the fall, right?" Steel nodded. "So I'll see you there."

"The thing of it is . . . I'm not supposed to tell you this . . . but my father said our family may have to change our names and stuff. Move to someplace and start all over. This gang . . . they're arresting them, but they're not sure they'll get them all. And even though this Grym guy isn't talking, my father says I could be at risk."

"Like witness protection?" she said, sounding excited.

"That kind of thing. Yeah."

"So when I see you at a science challenge, I'll pretend I don't know you."

"That would be good. I think. But not really."

"Other people don't need to know."

"Exactly."

"But we know," she said. And the way she said it ran electricity down his legs and out his toes.

"Yeah, we know."

"We're a good team."

"We are," he agreed.

"And Cairo, of course."

"Of course."

She giggled. Her nose scrunched up when she laughed. He hadn't noticed that before.

Kaileigh and Miss Kay took off across the station, with Kaileigh looking over her shoulder and meeting eyes with Steel, scrunching that same way again. He knew she was laughing, and that made him feel good inside.

"Ready to go home?" his mother asked.

"I suppose," he answered. "Wherever home turns out to be."

"Life's an adventure," she said.

With Cairo following on a trolley drawn by a haggard old man with big ears, they headed out into the parking lot, looking for their car, and the life they'd left behind.